WHITE RIVER WOLVES

ALANNA'S CALLING

DAWN SULLIVAN

Published by Dawn Sullivan

Cover Design: Dana Leah- Designs By Dana

Photographer: Shelton Cole- SC Photo

Model: Christina Gragg

Editors: CP Bialois and Jamie White

Language: English

For Christina a/k/a Care Bear. Thank you for being the sweet, kind, funny, supportive person you are.

RARE AND WHITE RIVER WOLVES READING ORDER

Nico's Heart- RARE Book 1
Phoenix's Fate- RARE Book 2
Josie's Miracle- White River Wolves Book 1
Trace's Temptation- RARE Book 3
Slade's Desire- White River Wolves Book 2
Saving Storm- RARE Book 4
Angel's Destiny- RARE Book 5
Janie's Salvation- White River Wolves Book 3
Sable's Fire- White River Wolves Book 4
Jaxson's Justice- RARE Book 6
Rikki's Awakening- RARE Book 7
Alanna's Calling- White River Wolves Book 5

1

Alanna Miller woke from a deep sleep to the sound of someone banging loudly on her apartment door. She froze, terror filling her at the first thought that came to her. *Her brother had found her.* Doug was here to take her home, back to the hell she'd endured for years before she'd been rescued by the White River Wolves.

"Alanna," a deep voice roared. "Open up!"

With a soft cry of fear, she sprang out of bed and to her feet, trying to figure out what to do. She couldn't return to the life she'd had before. The constant emotional and physical abuse. The name calling and degrading. The bruises, broken bones, pain and suffering. She'd been free of it for almost six months now. She felt safe, something she hadn't felt in so long; even before her parents passed away in a car accident twenty months ago and Doug took over as alpha of their sleuth.

She was finally able to be herself. Make her own decisions. Be… happy. Or as happy as she could be when she knew what the future held.

Not only that, but she had a purpose in life. A calling that couldn't go unanswered. She was meant to help others. To take away their pain. Heal them. Save them. She'd seen it in several visions and knew exactly what her reason for living was.

She'd even helped a couple of people in her new pack already. First, it was the alpha himself after he was kidnapped by the General's daughter, Ebony. Chase Montgomery had been taken, beaten daily, and then shot twice when protecting his mate's son, Jinx. He had mostly healed on his own by the time she saw him after the ordeal, but Alanna was able to take away all of his pain and discomfort. After everything he'd done for her, she was happy to have the chance to do something for him in return.

Then Alanna healed her new friend, Raven, who had been held by the General for a year. The poor dragoness was in constant agony after being hurt and experimented on for so long. Not to mention her time with a Colombian drug lord before that, who loved to terrorize and torture his prisoners. Helping Raven had put her down for a couple of weeks, suffering more than she would let anyone else know, but it was worth it. She regretted nothing.

It had felt so good to help Chase and Raven with her gift, and to know they not only appreciated it, but that she could trust them to keep her ability to heal others a secret. The only other person in her life Alanna had ever been able to place her trust in was her best friend, Fallon. A woman who was more of a sister to her than a friend.

Alanna had a gift. One she felt it was her destiny to use. People needed her, one person specifically. A little boy who just might be the one to end her existence, but she would go willingly if that happened. Her life for that of a child? She would pick a child every single time. But it wouldn't be for a while yet. She had time.

Time to help others in need. To live. To enjoy life.

At least, she thought she did. Alanna was never positive on the exact timeframe when visions came to her, but she was sure she had a few months left. Two or three if she were lucky. She could help a lot of people in that amount of time.

Alanna couldn't let her brother take her away from all the good she needed to do before her time on earth was over. She refused to allow him to.

Not only that, but she wasn't ready to leave *him*. The man who should have been the other half of her soul, but who would never claim her if what she'd seen in her visions came true. She wouldn't allow it. She couldn't. She refused to leave him alone in the world, shattered when he lost the one person who was supposed to be his world. His mate. And there was a very good chance that would happen.

While the vision of the child she would save someday was somewhat cloudy, she *knew* it was coming, and the outcome would very likely be death. Her death.

Unfortunately, no matter what she did, Alanna couldn't stop thinking of him, even though she knew he would never be hers. Dark hair, deep brown eyes with the most stunning flecks of green in them, and a cocky, sexy grin that took her breath away whenever she was lucky enough to catch a glimpse of it.

She'd spent the past five and a half months avoiding him, not wanting him to get the chance to scent her. Even in the very beginning when he came with the rest of the pack to rescue her from the hell she was enduring, he was never near enough to discover they were mates. At the time, it wasn't her doing. She didn't even realize that her mate was there. He was never near her when Chase and his team first made contact and they rode in separate vehicles on the way back to the pack lands. It wasn't until they arrived and she felt the connection to him when he exited the SUV he was in that she realized who he was to her. He was too far away to scent, but she *knew* him. Felt him. And every time after that when she saw him somewhere around the White River Wolves compound, she did everything she could to avoid him.

Alanna watched him from a distance. She couldn't help herself. If he was gone for any length of time, she listened closely to the others in the pack for news on him, absorbing everything about the gorgeous cat that she could. Even though they would never be together, she needed to know he was safe.

Her cat. A fierce tiger. One she had no doubt would protect her, would give his own life for her if it came down to it. She couldn't let that happen. While she was willing to die for the young boy in the future, there was no way she would put her mate in danger for anyone, no matter who they were. It was better to just keep her distance and never let him know who she was to him.

It probably would have been easier if she'd let the council place them somewhere else when she and Fallon were rescued, but she couldn't resist the chance to see him. To watch over him. Even if it was only for a short time. She just made sure she was very careful not to ever be near enough for him to inhale her scent. So far, it had worked. He seemed oblivious to what they were to each other. Sadly, he'd probably forgotten all about her after the rescue mission.

"Alanna!"

She was torn from her thoughts at the yelling of her name and the pounding that was getting louder. Alanna heard Fallon moving around in the bedroom next to hers, which was enough to break her from her thoughts and make her realize it couldn't be her brother at the door. There was no way he would be knocking if it was. Not with the entire apartment building full of shifters who would do everything within their power to protect her since she was now a part of their pack.

"Alanna, please, I need you! Please!"

There was so much pain and desperation in the voice this time and shock raced through her when she finally placed it. Phoenix Maddox of RARE. He was a complete alpha male. Not one to beg for anything. But here he was at her door, and now that she was finally wide awake and coherent, she could smell the overwhelming scent of his fear all the way in her bedroom.

It could only mean one thing.

Alanna was out of her bedroom and had the front door opened before Fallon made it to the living room. "Where is she?" she demanded, as she took in his haggard appearance.

Phoenix stared at her from dark green eyes full of agony and despair, tears streaming down his cheeks. "The hospital," he rasped. "It's the baby. Something's wrong with her. She… she isn't breathing."

Alanna didn't wait to hear more. Ignoring the fact that she was dressed in just her sleep shorts, a tank top with her favorite superhero on it, and no shoes, she raced out of the apartment.

No! This couldn't be happening! This wasn't something she'd foreseen. All she'd ever felt was peace and happiness from the baby whenever she was near Serenity. A love already building for the parents who talked to her daily. For the daddy who sang to her, and the mommy who read her books at night. No duress. No struggling. Nothing to make Alanna suspect there was any issue with the child at all.

She was aware of Phoenix right behind her, but she didn't take the time to say anything else. She was running up the hospital stairs and clearing the doors within two minutes. Alanna didn't even pause when she saw what appeared to be Phoenix's team, along with several others, in the waiting room.

There was a loud, keening wail coming from the back of the building; the sound of a mother crying out for her child. Alanna's heart jumped in her chest as she streaked past the receptionist area, her long, brunette hair flowing out behind her.

"Wait! You can't go back there!"

Not bothering to respond, Alanna continued down the hall and pushed open the doors to the Emergency Room. Serenity lay in a hospital bed, clutching tightly to Angel, her eyes glued to where Doc Josie was doing everything she could to save her daughter's life. Chase stood off to the side, his clear blue eyes dark with worry, his gaze also on the baby.

Alanna could feel the doctor's panic and helplessness as she barked out orders to her nurses, but the woman never stopped fighting. Unfortunately, she knew nothing the doctor did now would save the little one's life. Her spirit was already preparing to leave her body. She could see the pure white essence of it as it began to shimmer and rise.

Alanna had seen something like this before. At the time, she'd been unable to try and help the man who was one of her brother's enforcers. Someone who challenged Doug for his title as alpha and lost. He died an agonizing death; one she'd had to sit and watch, unsure anything she did would save him even if two other enforcers hadn't been holding her back. Not only that, but her brother didn't know the extent of her healing abilities. She'd kept as much from him as possible when it came to her gifts. If she'd tried to help the man and succeeded, who knew what Doug would have done to her.

She'd watched as the enforcer took his final breath, and a few minutes later his spirit left his body. It wasn't the pure white light of the baby in front of her, but had more of a tarnished, tan color to it. Still, that tan light rose to the heavens above, until there was nothing left to see after the Gods accepted him.

Alanna refused to sit back and watch the same thing happen to Phoenix and Serenity's daughter. She might not have had a choice before because of her brother, but she did now. She was going to fight like hell to give that little girl the future she deserved. Alanna had known for years now that there was a huge possibility she would give her own life for that of a child's. She just didn't expect it to be *this* child.

There was another one out there. A little boy who needed her, who may not be given the same chance at living that Alanna was about to give this baby. That thought broke her heart, but she couldn't think about it right now. There wasn't time.

Crossing the room, Alanna laid a hand on Josie's arm, squeezing it gently. When the doctor barely spared her a glance, she said, "You've done all you can do, Doc. It's my turn now."

Doc Josie's eyes widened, filling with tears as she shook her head. "No. I won't give up! I can do this!"

"Give me the child," Alanna said quietly, blocking out the sound of Serenity's harsh sobs. Phoenix had come to her for help, and she was going to give it to him. It didn't matter what anyone else in the room thought.

"Alanna, no, it's too much to ask," Angel cut in, her voice filled with apprehension.

"Angel..."

"No, Phoenix. It could kill her!"

"Angel's right," Chase said, moving over to put his arm around his mate. "I don't know how Alanna's gift works, but I do know that she was down for weeks after helping Raven. It could kill her."

"If she doesn't help, my baby will die!" The words were torn from Phoenix's throat as he held Serenity close.

"Let me!" Serenity cried, reaching for the little girl. "Let me save her. I can do it!"

"You can't, mate," Phoenix rasped, his voice heavy with sorrow. "You're too weak after having her. I can't lose you both."

Ignoring it all, Alanna stepped forward and slid her arms under the baby's still body. Lifting her gently, she walked over to a chair in the corner of the room and sat. Placing the little girl's chest over hers so they were heart to heart and lowered her head and closed her eyes.

It took a moment, but then she heard the faint beat, showing her the baby was still alive. She was a fighter and she wanted to live, but was in so much pain. Blocking out everything around her, Alanna focused on that heartbeat. She felt a peace enter her that came without fail, right before the healing began and the pain hit.

She always told people when they asked if it hurt her to use her gift that what she felt was nothing like the pain the person she was healing endured. It was a lie, worded in a way no one would be able to scent the acrid smell of it. Technically, it really wasn't anything like the pain they were feeling… it was so much worse. The thing was, it never hit her hard right away. It would creep up slowly, and then consume her about an hour or so later. After that, she would be down for days, in blinding agony. Stuck in darkness and horror, unable to communicate even though she was aware of what was going on around her, until she was finally able to claw her way out.

Not even Fallon knew how much she suffered. It was the only lie she'd ever told her best friend because she knew the other woman wouldn't be able to handle the full truth.

"You don't have to do this, Alanna."

Alanna heard Chase, but she didn't acknowledge him. Her full attention was now on the baby and keeping the little one tied to earth.

Sweet baby, she whispered from her mind to the child's as she flooded her with love and healing power, *it isn't your time just yet. You are needed here, with your parents, and all of the ones who love you. You have a purpose, a destiny to fulfill.*

The first thing she needed to do was to somehow get

the baby's spirit back fully into her body. To accomplish that, she was going to have to lessen the terrible pain she could feel surrounding the child. It was everywhere, starting with the way her skin was so sensitive to anything that touched it. It was hot, with pinpricks of agony everywhere. And then there was the way her heart felt as if it was being squeezed tightly in her chest, causing unbearable agony. The way her lungs almost felt as if they were being crushed, which would explain why she couldn't pull air into them.

There was so much misery and suffering. The little one was struggling to choose to fight for a life with her parents or to move on into the afterlife. As far as Alanna was concerned, there wasn't a choice. The child was meant to be a warrior like her father someday. Protecting the innocent and saving the ones who could not save themselves. Failure was not an option.

That excruciating pain had to go. Now.

Taking a deep breath, Alanna opened herself up fully to the child, stifling a moan when the first bout of fear and agony touched her. The baby was terrified, hurting so much she was ready to just let go. Reaching for a peace that was being promised to her from the Gods above.

Let me help you, little one. Let me lessen the pain; take it all away if I can. I will fight for you, but you must fight for yourself as well.

Gritting her teeth together tightly, Alanna began the process of absorbing the child's torturous pain into her own body. It was horrible, like sharp shards of glass being shoved into her chest. Searing blades slicing into her skin. Her heart stuttering as an invisible fist seemed to close around it.

Alanna fought through it all, blocking out everything except drawing the pain from the tiny baby to herself. The more Alanna took from her, the more the child's will to live returned, and tears flooded her eyes when the heart-beat next to hers began to pick up and a breath filled the small chest.

"Oh my God!" she heard someone gasp. "It's working. Whatever she's doing, it's working."

Alanna ran a hand gently down the child's back as she began to push healing energy into her small body. At the same time, she kept absorbing her pain, refusing to leave any of it behind. She would handle the fallout from it later, but the baby girl had been through enough. If Alanna died, so be it, but the child would start her new journey in life happy and pain free.

We are so proud of you, little bear.

Alanna stiffened at the voice in her head, something she wasn't used to hearing even though she'd had the gift of telepathy all her life, but didn't pause in her act of heal-ing. *Who are you?*

Who I am is not important, except for the fact that I am one of the Gods above that you pray to at night. We are here, and we hear your prayers, Alanna.

Swallowing hard, Alanna closed her eyes and lowered her head, resting it softly against the baby's. *If you are who you say you are, then please, answer my prayer now and save this sweet child in my arms. It is not time for you to take her.*

You are right, Alanna Miller, it is not Nevaeh's time to join us, and it will not be for many years to come. She has her own destiny to follow, as all of you do. A large and important one to your pack.

Alanna's breath hitched in her throat, and she concentrated on removing that last little bit of pain from the baby, as she whispered, *Thank you, Goddess.*

You are welcome, my child.

As the Goddess slipped out of her mind, the baby let out a loud cry, her small body shuddering. Alanna opened her eyes to see the white light of Nevaeh's spirit merging back with her as the sounds of her cries filled the room.

When she was sure she'd taken all of the little one's pain and swamped her with enough healing power to completely heal her heart and lungs, Alanna broke contact with Nevaeh, struggling to hide the agony she was feeling so no one else would know.

A tremulous smile crossed her lips, as she slowly rose to her feet and made her way over to where Phoenix and Serenity were staring at her in wonder and shock.

"You did it," Serenity whispered, reaching out for her child. "You saved our baby."

"Little Nevaeh is ready for you to hold her now, Mama," Alanna whispered, placing the child gently in Serenity's arms and smiling at a worried, awestruck Phoenix who stood close to her.

"Nevaeh?"

Alanna nodded, giving her a gentle smile. "Yes, Nevaeh. It means Heaven. You daughter is a gift from the Heavens, and the Gods have chosen her name for her."

Serenity's eyes widened in shock as her gaze went from Alanna to her daughter. "They did?"

"Yes," Alanna whispered, taking a step back as the pain and agony in her body threatened to take over. It felt as if the fiery flames of hell were skating over her skin, a dark pressure pushing on her chest. She had just cheated death by saving Nevaeh, and now Alanna was going to find out if she would take the child's place.

"Alanna, let me help you," Doc Josie said, reaching for her.

Alanna shook her head, stepping back quickly before Josie's hand could connect with her. There was no way she would be able to handle the feel of someone's touch on her skin right now. She had to get out of there.

"I'm fine, but thank you, doctor." Turning back to the parents, she gave them a soft smile. "Your daughter has an important destiny to follow. She will be a fierce warrior like her father, with a big, loving heart like her mother." She glanced over at the White River Wolves alphas. "She will be very important to this pack, Alphas." An image hit her suddenly, a vision of the future, and a larger smile spread across her face. "And very important to you and your family."

After one last look at the precious bundle Serenity held close to her, Alanna turned and left the room. Her vision was beginning to blur and the darkness was starting to take over. It wouldn't be much longer before she wasn't able to function. She needed to get home before that happened.

Alanna didn't hear Angel's cry of dismay or see Chase rush toward her when the darkness hit her full force, putting her to her knees. Didn't hear her own screams of agony that tore from her chest when he lifted her into his arms.

All she knew was darkness, torment, and severe, excruciating torture as what she'd been struggling to prevent happening in front of others took place, and there wasn't a damn thing she could do about it.

2

Trigger raked a hand through his thick, dark hair as the SUV pulled up to the gates of the White River Wolves compound. He was exhausted. They'd spent the past four days tracking down a rogue wolf shifter for the council and he was running on very little sleep. All he wanted to do was go find his bed and crash for a full twenty-four hours. Well, after he checked on a certain brown-haired, chocolate-eyed beauty who he had no doubt would haunt his dreams just like every other time he closed his eyes.

For some reason, the cute little female seemed to be avoiding him. He'd had no idea she was his when they rescued her from her deranged brother. He was never close to her on the mission, not even when they arrived back to the compound in different vehicles. River had parked the one they were in near the apartments, and even though he'd seen the adorable bear, that was as far as it went. But a few weeks later, he started noticing the most tantalizing scent around the compound. Every time he tried to follow it, he came up empty, until a couple of months ago when he saw her leave Raven's hospital room.

He'd been walking down the hall after stopping by the hospital to check on a young enforcer, Zane, who'd managed to almost slice his finger off when sparring with another enforcer who was still in training. He'd never gotten the full story, but the female had taken offense to something Zane said or did and decided to handle it herself instead of going up the chain of command. While she should have come to him or Slade, Trigger chose to let it go because he couldn't say that he blamed her. Zane had a big fucking mouth and needed to be taken down a peg or two.

Trigger had just turned the corner to go down another hallway when the little bear slipped out of one of the rooms in front of him. He'd stood frozen in shock when her scent hit him, unable to say a word as it washed over him and somehow seemed to settle the beast within; something no one in his life had ever been able to do. Not even himself.

He'd seen her before, of course. Had her in sight on his rifle when her brother was growling at her, and wanted to put a bullet into the bastard's brain when he threatened her. But at the time, he'd had no idea the breath-taking, curvy little bear was his mate.

Trigger would have spoken to Alanna in the hospital, but she'd rushed down the hall without acknowledging his own scent, or even glancing back. And then... he'd heard what was being said in the room she'd just left. His woman, his beautiful mate, had somehow just taken away all the pain from Jaxson's mate, Raven. She'd removed it and healed Raven, leaving her mostly pain free.

Trigger was still trying to wrap his mind around RARE's psychic abilities at the time, and the thought of his mate having a gift like theirs stunned him. He was unable to follow her from the hospital, not sure what to say or do, so he held back and watched her from afar. That's when he noticed she was doing the same with him. It was obvious Alanna knew he was hers, but for some reason wasn't ready for him to find out.

Trigger decided at that time that he would play her game for a while longer. Give her whatever space it was that she thought she needed, while he continued to try and wrap his mind around the fact that she could somehow heal others... or at least take their pain. He wasn't exactly sure what it was that she did, and wasn't comfortable asking anyone else. When he was ready, he would get his answers from the person who should be the one to give them to him. His mate.

What he did know was that after she helped Raven, Alanna didn't leave her apartment for weeks. It came to a point where he was about to knock on her damn door and check on her when he overheard a conversation between Jackson and another member of RARE, and learned that something had happened to his mate when she healed Raven. She suffered from it, in pain and unable to move, and there was nothing anyone could do for her.

When Trigger heard that, he'd immediately left the room and headed to her apartment, but when he went to cross the street to get to her building, she walked out the front door with Fallon. They'd turned away from him and walked toward the park and he'd followed for a few minutes. Only when he was sure she was okay did he slip off and head out into the forest of trees beyond the compound. Stripping, he'd shifted into his tiger and ran for hours until he was finally able to get his emotions under control.

His mate had a special gift, one he had been unable to fully comprehend, and was still having issues with it if he were honest. One that hurt her when she used it. That kept her confined to her apartment, to her bed, in pain for who the fuck knew how long. One that she chose to use to help others no matter what it did to her. Raven was proof of that. How could he keep her safe from something like that?

"I'm not entirely sure what's going on. All I know is that Phoenix ran out of the hospital like it was on fire, went to the apartment building, and not long after he came back with Alanna. I haven't seen anyone since."

Trigger stiffened, immediately tuning into the conversation between Tyler, the enforcer at the gate, and Sable.

"Oh shit," Sable whispered. "I wonder if Serenity went into labor and there was an issue."

"I have no idea," Tyler said, shaking his head as he opened the gate, "but whatever is happening, it isn't good. Alanna was moving so fast I don't think her feet touched the ground."

"It was the baby," Charlotte interjected, as Sable waived to Tyler and pulled into the compound. Trigger glanced over to see she was on her phone. "Something was wrong with the birth. She wasn't breathing."

"Oh, God," Sable whispered as she stepped on the gas, driving straight to the hospital.

"How is Alanna involved?" Trigger ground out, barely holding onto the anger that was suddenly flooding through him. His mate was in danger. He knew it. Somehow, she was going to try to save the baby's life, putting her own at risk.

"I don't know," Sable whispered, but he scented the lie in the air. She knew, just as he did.

"Bullshit," he growled, low and deadly. He had never felt the kind of fury he was feeling at the moment. It was all consuming, and threatening to take over and make him do something he might regret later. Alanna was his mate, dammit. His to protect, and there was no doubt in his mind that she was in danger right now.

Sable came to a stop in front of the large building, turning to look at him, her eyes widening at whatever she saw. "Trigger…"

Unable to contain his rage any longer, Trigger let out a roar as he slammed his fist into the dashboard, leaving a huge dent in it and breaking open the skin on his knuckles.

"She is in there trying to save that child's life," he snarled. "Probably at the expense of her own. While I know how precious a baby's life is, *that* is unacceptable. Her life is just as important as anyone else's! She is just as fucking precious!"

Trigger was out of the SUV and striding across the lawn before anyone in the vehicle could comment. He took the stairs two at a time and entered the front doors, taking in the scene at a glance.

The entire RARE team, along with their mates and other members of the pack, were in the waiting room. There were so many of them that they spilled out into the main entrance as well. Trigger's gaze raked over their worried, upset expressions before he ignored them all and inhaled deeply, searching for the only person who mattered at that time.

He could hear a baby's cries coming from the end of the hall and around the corner, and quickly made his way in that direction, a low growl emerging when he finally scented his mate. Just as he was almost at a door with a sign that said Emergency at the top of it, the door opened, Chase emerging with Alanna in his arms.

Trigger quickly closed the gap between them, his chest now vibrating deeply with growls as he bared his fangs. His claws burst free of his fingertips, and he had to bite back a roar that wanted to escape.

She was so pale and still, if Trigger wasn't able to hear the steady beat of her heart he would've thought she was dead. That thought made him want to kill. Everyone.

"Give her to me," he demanded, sliding his arms under Alanna. When Chase looked as if he were going to argue, Trigger snarled, "Give me my mate, Alpha."

Chase's eyes narrowed on him, his lips curling up as he flashed his fangs. "Watch how you speak to me, son."

Doc Josie rushed out of the room and motioned to Chase. "Hurry, Chase. You can argue about that later. Give Alanna to Trigger. We need to get her in a room and try to make her comfortable until I can figure out how to help her."

"There isn't anything you can do," a soft voice said, as Trigger gathered his bear in his arms. He looked back to see Alanna's friend Fallon making her way down the hall toward them. "This happens when she uses her abilities, and depending on how bad it was, it can put her under for a while."

"How bad was it?" Trigger demanded, glaring at the doctor and alpha. He knew he should tone it down. Chase saved his life over twenty years ago, taking him and his mother in when their entire streak was destroyed. The alpha gave him the chance to make something of himself, guiding him off the destructive path he'd been on and pointing him onto a much better one. He would always be grateful to him, but right now Trigger was having a hard time remembering that when his mate lay almost lifeless in his arms.

"Bad," Phoenix said, stepping out into the hall with them, a grave look in his eyes. "My daughter was dying. Alanna…" he paused, swallowing hard as his eyes misted over with tears. "Alanna saved her life. Brought her back from near death somehow. I have no idea how."

Trigger's arms tightened around his woman as he stared at the people in front of him, his body pulsing with rage. "You knew after she helped Raven what it does to her."

"Yes," Phoenix said quietly, not bothering to deny it.

"You knew she was down for weeks after she took Raven's pain. All of you knew."

"Fuck, man. Yeah, we did, but I couldn't let my daughter die."

"But you were okay with exchanging her life for my mate's?" Trigger growled, baring his fangs at the wolf. He was so fucking pissed. It was a good thing he held Alanna in his arms, or he would have already shifted and attacked the bastard who thought it was okay to trade his mate's life for anyone else's.

Trigger heard the sharp intake of breath and his gaze went past Phoenix to where Serenity held her daughter, who was now sleeping peacefully in her arms.

"I am so sorry," Serenity whispered, and Trigger could hear the sorrow in her voice. "We didn't know what else to do."

"No, but you knew Alanna wouldn't turn you down." He glanced down at his kind bear with a heart bigger than anyone he knew. He'd seen it in the way she treated the others in their pack. How she was with the mothers at the park, helping them with their children. The way she always asked others how they were doing and actually took the time to listen to their replies. When she went out of her way to help Raven, knowing what it would cost her. She was always giving to others, never asking for anything in return. "I'm taking her home. Fallon, you're welcome to come. The rest of you, it would be in your best interest to stay far away from me until my mate is healed."

Not waiting for a reply, Trigger turned on his heel and walked away, not looking back when Chase called his name. He was being unreasonable, and he knew it. No one made Alanna save the child. She'd made the decision on her own, and he couldn't fault her for it. It was just tearing him up inside to know that she was hurting, and there wasn't a damn thing he could do about it.

He walked past the waiting room, not bothering to acknowledge the men and women who stood silently watching him. He had nothing to say to any of them. He had one purpose, and that was to take care of the precious woman he held. Everyone else could fuck right off at the moment.

All that mattered was his mate.

3

Alanna couldn't breathe. The pain in her chest was almost too much to bear. It was crushing her, and her heart felt like it was going to burst apart. She'd never felt so much agony in her life. She wanted to cry, to scream, but couldn't seem to make a sound. The darkness was swamping her, pushing down on her harder than it ever had before.

She knew why she was hurting, why she felt as if she were suffocating, unable to take a breath. She always remembered when she healed someone, who it was and what it entailed, but it didn't change the fact that she was going through the aftermath of it. Knowing who and why didn't help. She still suffered.

Alanna wasn't just scared, she was terrified. What she was experiencing this time was so much worse than anything she'd ever gone through before. She was afraid the Gods above would be coming for her soon, ready to take her into the afterlife, and she wasn't ready to leave this world yet. She was supposed to have more time. To heal more people. To save the little boy who needed her. To watch over her mate from afar.

"It's going to be all right, daughter. It's all going to be okay."

Daughter? The voice was soft and soothing, but Alanna couldn't place who it belonged to. The pain was too much. She couldn't concentrate.

"Tell me again what happens when she gets like this, Fallon."

Fallon was there. That was good. Her friend would know what to do. Or what not to do, as the case may be. There wasn't much that could be done right now. It would be a waiting game on their end. Alanna would just have to suffer through the hell she was in and pray she was still alive in the end.

"There isn't much we can do," Fallon whispered, and Alanna hated the anguish she heard in the other woman's voice. This wasn't the first time she'd gone through an episode after a healing with Alanna. She knew what to expect, but it was obvious it still upset her. "Alanna told me when she's like this, her body becomes heavy. Leaden. She can't move. Can't eat. I try to push fluids in her, but it's really difficult because it's hard for her to swallow." There was silence, and then, "I've never seen her this bad before. She is so still and pale. I can see the pain etched into her face." Her breath hitched and she sobbed, "She's hurting so much, isn't she?"

Alanna flinched when a loud roar filled the room, followed by a crash, and then a snarled, "Son of a bitch!"

"You need to get control of your cat, son, or leave."

"I will not leave my mate." The words were said in a deep growl, the voice low and full of rage.

"You're going to scare her."

Alanna pushed through the pain as she listened, realization hitting her as they spoke. She knew that voice. That deep, sexy tenor. She'd never had it aimed at her, but heard him talking with others in the past.

Her tiger was here. In the same room as her. And he knew about them.

It didn't make sense. She would never allow herself to be anywhere near him, let alone in the same room.

She was so confused. She remembered healing little Nevaeh, and then saying she was going home. How did she end up here... wherever here was.

"Fuck. I don't want to scare her, but I'm having a hard time controlling my cat."

He sounded so upset. Worried. Maybe even a little scared himself. She didn't like him feeling like that. He was always so calm and controlled. Sometimes teasing and laughing. But never like this.

"Shift. Go for a run and get your head on straight. I will watch over your mate until you get back."

No! She didn't want him to leave! Alanna fought to move. To open her eyes. To speak. Anything to get his attention. She needed him there. She was terrified. Not of him, but of the fact that she was struggling to breathe. That it felt as if someone were sitting on her chest and it was going to crush her.

"Mama..."

"Go. I promise to take care of her."

No! Dammit, no, he couldn't go. She needed him.

"Something's wrong," Fallon said urgently, and Alanna felt the gentle touch of her friend's fingertips against her forehead. The skin-to-skin contact hurt, but she was grateful for it anyway. It helped her feel connected to someone else in the room.

A small whimper slipped out as Alanna managed to pry her eyes open. Stark agony slammed through her head and she moaned, tears sliding out and down her cheeks.

"Oh, God! Alanna! You're awake!"

As hard as she tried, Alanna couldn't move. Her vision was blurry, and her head ached fiercely. Her eyelids fluttered closed, but she pried them back open, causing another whimper to break free as she was once again swamped with pain.

"Hush, daughter, you are safe. Everything's going to be all right."

There was that word again. Daughter. Her parents had passed away almost two years ago. And even when her mother was alive, she'd never spoken to Alanna in that soft, loving tone. They didn't have the type of relationship she'd seen between other mothers and their children. Her mother was distant, hiding behind a façade that masked sorrow and anger, stuck in an unhappy marriage with a controlling man who was not her true mate. And her father, he was just an ass. However, while he never physically hurt her the way her brother did, he never stopped Doug from doing it either.

Alanna moaned, her breath coming out in small pants. It hurt like crazy, but at least she was breathing. For a while there, she'd really thought she might not have a choice on if she stayed on earth, or if her spirit would rise to the heavens.

"Alanna, what do you need?"

More tears trickled out, and she could feel them as

they moved across her skin. How could she tell them what she needed? How could she make them understand?

"I can't fucking stand this!" her mate snarled. "I've got to get out of here before I tear down the whole damn house."

No! No! No!

Screams erupted from her throat, muffled by the fact that her mouth felt like it was wired shut, and her eyes blinked wildly as she struggled to get words out. She needed him *there.* With her.

"Wait!" Fallon cried, and Alanna felt her friend's fingertips skate across her forehead once again. "I could be wrong, but I think she wants you to stay, Trigger." When her screams began to lessen at Fallon's words, Fallon whispered, "Is that what it is, Alanna? You don't want Trigger to leave?"

Alanna blinked rapidly, only stopping when the pain became too much, but she didn't close her eyes. The darkness was coming for her again. She knew she didn't have much time. But she refused to succumb to it until she knew her mate was staying.

There was movement above her, and then that handsome face that she'd come to care so much for was there. It was blurry, but she could still make out his features. Ones she'd memorized a long time ago.

"Alanna?"

He was so close, if she wasn't stuck in the damn position she was in she would've been able to reach out and touch him. She wanted to trace her fingers over that scowl on his forehead, smooth away the lines between his captivating eyes. She never thought she would be this close to him. Closing her eyes, she inhaled, a sense of calm filling her when his scent surrounded her.

The pain was still there, just as horrible as it was before, but for some reason having her mate near made it easier to handle. She opened her eyes again to look at him, the small whimpers slowly fading away.

When she suddenly lost sight of him, a cry rose up in her throat and he was instantly back. "I'm right here, sweet mate. I'm not going anywhere." His eyes never leaving hers, he said, "Mama, can you get me a chair so I can sit by Alanna?"

He was staying. Thanks to Fallon, her mate was going to stay by her side where she really needed him. She already owed the woman for contacting the council and getting them to send Chase and his team to rescue her from the situation with her brother. Also, for leaving North Carolina with her, and agreeing to settle with the White River Wolves in Colorado. Now, it seemed she owed her friend for more.

Alanna listened as a chair was placed next to the bed she lay in, and then Trigger lowered himself down into it. He was right next to her, but she felt her fear rising again. She hated it. While his scent was still all around her, comforting her, she couldn't see him. She *needed* to be able to see him. She had no idea what was wrong with her. For months she'd avoided him whenever possible, looking out for him, not wanting to break his heart in the future. Now, none of that seemed to matter. She couldn't stand having him out of her sight.

When Alanna began to whimper softly again, Trigger reached over and enveloped her hand in one of his large ones. He was so gentle, but her skin felt like it was on fire and it still hurt. Hell, everything hurt, but it didn't matter. She would choose his touch any day and suffer through the pain.

"She can't see you, son."

"What?"

"I think she's upset because she can't see you."

"She can't move," Fallon said quietly. "She won't be able to turn her head in your direction."

"Shit." Trigger stood so he was in her line of sight again. "I'm sorry, sweet mate. I wasn't thinking."

Alanna's eyes clung to his as she slowly began to calm again. Just being able to see him made that feeling of safety return. It somehow slowed her racing pulse and helped ease the fear inside.

She felt her brow pull into a slight frown as she noticed the fatigue on her mate's face. He'd been gone for a few days, probably saving someone's life like he had hers. He looked exhausted, and she didn't like it.

"I have an idea," Fallon murmured, as she moved so Alanna could see her. "What if Trigger sits in the chair, and we tilt your head so you can see him, Alanna. Would that be okay?"

Alanna blinked her eyes rapidly for a moment, and then stopped. Yes, that could work. It would hurt like hell, but she would deal with it. He needed to rest.

"What if it causes her more pain?" Trigger asked, watching her in concern.

Alanna blinked again.

"I think that is a risk she is willing to take."

Trigger growled and a shiver ran through her when the side of his top lip curled up to show a pearly white fang. Mates were known to be possessive and protective, but she didn't think she'd ever see her mate act that way with her. She found that it made her feel cared for. Special. Something she'd never felt before. "She needs to stop taking fucking risks. I don't like seeing her in pain."

"None of us do," Fallon said, letting out a soft sigh. "Now sit." When Trigger growled again, Fallon snapped, "Look, the sooner you sit your ass in that chair, the sooner my friend can pass the hell out so she doesn't feel the pain for a few hours."

"What do you mean?" Trigger's mom asked softly.

"Trust me, I know Alanna. She is fighting it, but she needs to rest. She won't do that until she knows Trigger is okay first."

"Because she always puts everyone else first," Trigger snarled, showing those large fangs again.

"Exactly. And it's obvious how tired you are. If I can see it, she can. Now, please sit."

Alanna fought back another whimper when her mate left her sight again, and then clenched her teeth tightly together when Fallon placed her hands on the sides of Alanna's head and turned her slowly.

"Fuck, I can smell how much pain she's in. I hate it."

"I'm so glad I don't have your sense of smell," Fallon told them quietly as she ran a hand softly down Alanna's long hair. "I would have to scent whatever you are every time Alanna did something like this. I don't know if I could handle that."

Alanna watched her mate's eyes darken and he snarled, "That shit is going to stop. She is not going to keep putting herself in danger the way she has been. I won't allow it."

Fallon laughed. "Good luck with that."

"I don't need luck."

"Look, Trigger," Fallon interrupted, "you need to realize something fast. Alanna is kind and compassionate. She would do almost anything for anyone if she had the power to, but she has a backbone of steel. You aren't going to be able to stop her from healing others any better than I can. She says it is her calling, and it's something she fully believes in. The only thing you can do is support her."

Trigger's jaw hardened, his eyes flashing as his cat made a quick appearance. He looked like he was going argue, but instead he shook his head and leaned forward to place a gentle kiss on Alanna's forehead. "Get some sleep, my mate."

When he leaned back in the chair, still holding her hand in his, Alanna allowed her eyes to slowly drift shut and let the darkness take over. She was exhausted and needed to escape the pain for a while. She would worry about everything else later.

4

"I don't care who you are, you are not coming into my house."

His mother's voice woke him and instantly put Trigger on alert. She sounded angry, and Sharina Michelson angry was not a good thing. She was just under six feet tall with flashing amber eyes, fiery golden-red curls that went to her waist, and a temper to match. She wasn't one to sit back and stay quiet. If she felt a certain way about something, everyone in the entire room would know. And she didn't back down from what she believed in. Ever.

"I just want to check on Alanna and make sure she's okay. Angel and I accepted her into the pack. She's our responsibility."

"Not anymore, Alpha. My son brought his mate home to me to take care of and protect. That is exactly what I'm going to do. She is ours now, and we do not need your help."

"She doesn't need protection from us, Sharina."

"Obviously, she does." Trigger's mom's voice rose as

she spat out, "If she didn't, she wouldn't be lying in bed right now unable to move. She wouldn't be screaming from pain. Crying because it hurts to breathe."

"I'm not the one who asked her to save the child's life, tigress."

"No, but you didn't stop it either, did you?" Sharina growled, her voice shaking with fury. "Now, get the hell off my front porch and don't come back without an invitation."

"Sharina..."

"That sweet bear is my son's mate. That makes her my daughter, Chase Montgomery. My family. And I will always protect my family no matter the cost. Now, go!"

Trigger rose slowly from the chair when he heard Chase's low growl of warning. He needed to be ready to step in if his mother needed him, although that was highly unlikely. The sixty-five-year-old Siberian tigress could hold her own.

"I'll go now, Sharina, but it would be good for both you and your son to remember who is alpha of this pack. Think next time before you challenge me. I may not be so forgiving. Also, remember who took you both in when you had nowhere to go. Who gave you a huge family, one who loves and cares for you, just as I do."

"Trust me, I haven't forgotten what happened to my streak, Alpha. I was there. I watched as my husband, parents, and grandparents were murdered. Nor have I forgotten the home you gave us afterwards. But that doesn't change the fact that all of you put my son's mate in danger last night. She almost died. There's a chance she still could. Know now, if that happens, Trigger and I will leave this place because I know he will never be able to forgive you, and neither will I."

"Sharina..."

There was the sound of the door slamming shut, and then silence.

Trigger raised his arms above his head, stretching his back. Glancing at his watch, he saw that it was almost noon. He'd been sleeping in that uncomfortable as hell straight-back chair, with his head resting on his arms on the bed for a good seven hours, and he was feeling it. Bending over, he leaned down until he almost touched the floor. Then he stretched one arm behind his back, and then the other.

"You're awake."

Trigger glanced over to where his mother stood in the doorway, but it wasn't him she was speaking to. Her eyes were on the woman in the bed beside him. He looked down, stifling a growl when he saw that she didn't appear to be feeling any better than the night before. Fallon had warned them that it could take weeks for Alanna to get better, but he was hoping to see some improvement this morning.

Her eyes were clouded over with pain, and when she whimpered softly he quickly moved over to sit in the chair again. "Hey there, beautiful. I just woke up, too. Had to stretch some of the kinks out. I'm back now."

As he was talking, there was a knock on the front door. He inhaled deeply, but couldn't smell much beyond his mate and the intense agony that was rolling off her. She was miserable, and it drove him fucking crazy that he couldn't help her.

"That should be Doc Josie," Sharina said, smiling over at them. "I'll be right back."

A low growl began to rumble in Trigger's chest and he rose, moving to stand in front of his mate. The doctor was at the hospital last night. Granted, she'd been trying to help Alanna when he arrived, but she'd been there when Alanna saved the baby's life. There was no doubt in his mind that Josie knew what it would do to his mate. How it would hurt her. Maybe not to the extent that it had, but she knew. He didn't want the doc anywhere near his woman.

His mother entered the room first, cautiously, because she had to have known he was about to lose his shit. Doc Josie followed very slowly behind her, stopping in the doorway, a black doctor's bag in one hand. Her eyes were full of concern, but also trepidation. Good, he wanted her to be nervous around him.

"Trigger, she's only here because I called her."

"Why?" he demanded, glaring over at his mother. "Why the fuck would you do that after what happened?"

"Because Alanna needs her help," Sharina said in a soft, coaxing tone. "Just for a few minutes. Then she will leave."

"No." His tone was cold and hard. He didn't want the doctor anywhere near his mate.

"Trigger..."

"No."

"Trigger, please," Doc Josie interjected, holding out a hand as if in peace. "I know I screwed up last night. I couldn't save Nevaeh. No matter how hard I tried, I couldn't save her." She winced, her eyes clouding over as she whispered, "I know I should have said something, done something to stop Alanna, but I wasn't thinking clearly at the time. All I could think about was saving Phoenix and Serenity's baby."

"You knew what it would do to her," he said harshly. "What it would cost her."

She nodded slowly. "To a certain degree, yes." Her eyes went to where Alanna lay motionless behind him, and they misted with tears. A shudder ran through her body as her hand dropped to her side. "But I didn't know it would be like this. I can scent her pain. She's hurting so much. It's excruciating."

"Because she used her gift to save a child who was at death's door!" Trigger snarled, unable to hold back the anger he felt at the memory of the night before when he first saw her. So still and pale, in agony and unable to move. Not much had changed since then. "Which put her in danger of dying herself. Even if you didn't fully know, you had to at least suspect that she could have died."

Swallowing hard, Josie nodded as tears tracked down her face. "Yes, I did, but it was her choice, Trigger. It was one she made. I didn't make it for her. None of us did. Chase and Angel both told her she didn't have to do it."

"You should have stopped her!" he roared, his eyes flashing darkly, his tiger rising to the surface. The beast was wild inside him, full of rage. Wanting out to protect what was his. "Instead, you all took advantage of her kind, giving nature when I wasn't here to protect her!"

The soft whimpers coming from behind him was the only thing that kept him where he was. He wanted the doctor out of his house and away from his mate. He didn't want anyone near her except his mother and Fallon. It was so damn hard to hold his cat back.

"Trigger, I just want to help Alanna. Please." When he

bared his fangs at her, Josie held up a hand. "Ten minutes and I will leave. She needs an IV to help keep her hydrated over the next few days, possibly a feeding tube, and she needs a catheter put in. There's no other way for her to go to the bathroom unless you use bed pads, because if she can't control her body, it would stand to reason that she can't control her bodily functions as well."

Trigger stiffened as he realized he hadn't thought about how Alanna would use the restroom when she was stuck in bed and couldn't even move her head by herself. Shit. He could carry her to the bathroom, but that would cause his sweet bear a lot of agony. He didn't want that. It had been bad enough just tilting her head to the side so she could see him.

Turning, he knelt by the bed, locking his gaze with Alanna. Gently, he brushed a tear away that slipped from her painfilled, deep brown eyes. "Hey beautiful." She blinked once, her gaze clinging to his. "We are going to have to figure out a way to communicate. How about one blink for no, and two for yes?"

She blinked twice.

"Okay, we have a decision to make. As much as I want to take over and handle everything, I won't do that without your permission. And you don't know me well enough right now to allow that to happen. So, we are going to work together to get this all figured out. Sound good?"

Two blinks.

"We have two choices. One, I send someone to town to get you some bed pads or something since you won't be able to move for the near future." He stopped when she began to blink rapidly. Frowning, he struggled to understand what she was trying to tell him. "That's what you did before?" he guessed. "Bed pads? Fallon helped you by changing them?"

Two blinks.

"Okay, that is definitely an option then. Second option is to let Doc Josie put in a catheter." He leaned closer, and whispered, "I have absolutely no issue with helping you if you choose option one, and my mom was a nurse years ago. She would help too. But I think the second option may be better because you won't have to go through the pain of us moving you around to change out the pad. I hate the thought of you being in any more pain than you absolutely have to be."

She was slow to respond, but finally she blinked twice.

"So, option two?"

Two blinks.

"Okay, sweet mate. Would you like me to stay while the doc gets it ready?"

There was nothing. She just stared at him with wide eyes, a look of vulnerability in them that tore at his heart.

"Do you want me to stay?"

Nothing.

"Do you want me to leave?"

Alanna closed her eyes for a long moment.

Trigger brushed a piece of hair away from her face and leaned closer to whisper in her ear. "I can tell how terrified you are, mate. I don't know if it is because of the pain the procedure might cause, or if it is the thought of me not being here to protect you like I wasn't last night. Either way, I want to be here for you. I want to stay, if you'll let me. I won't look at what the doc is doing. I won't move from where I'm at right now. Won't take my eyes from yours."

He pulled back and watched her closely. She opened her eyes and slowly blinked twice.

"Thank you, Alanna." Not moving his gaze from hers like he promised, he raised his voice to say, "Doc Josie, my mate and I would appreciate it if you would put the IV and catheter in. As soon as you are done, you can go out to the kitchen and give my mother any instructions you might have. She was a nurse when we lived with our streak. She is more than capable of taking over after it's in place."

Doc Josie moved forward, opening the black bag she held. With Sharina's help, she moved the blankets and quickly and efficiently did what she needed to. Afterwards, she hesitated, but then turned and left the room without another word, his mother following closely behind her.

Trigger lowered his head, closed his eyes, and rested his cheek next to Alanna's in silence, reveling in the skin-to-skin contact. His heart that had been pounding in his chest from the moment Doc Josie walked into his house, finally began to calm, and his anger slowly dissipating. After a long moment, he gently kissed her cheek, and then her lips. "You did so good, sweetheart. Now, it's time for some more rest."

Alanna's gaze roamed over his face, as if making sure he was okay, and then her eyes slowly closed. Her dark brown lashes fluttered against her pale skin until she finally let go and drifted off to sleep.

Trigger stared at her for several more minutes before

he finally stood. Raking a hand through his hair, he let out a yawn. He was so tired.

"Go shower, son. I'll stay with her while you're gone."

"I can't leave her, Mama. She's scared."

"There are so many things for her to be terrified of right now, Trigger. I know it helps her having you near, but you will only be gone for a few minutes. Take a shower, grab something to eat, and come back."

Trigger hesitated, neither he nor his cat wanting to leave the beautiful woman who was coming to mean so much to them. He knew he needed to brush his teeth, take a shower, and put on clean clothes. But Alanna was his life now. His everything. And it was hard to walk away for any amount of time when he knew she would be afraid if she woke up and he was gone. Taking a deep breath, he finally capitulated. "I'll shower, but that's it. Ten minutes tops."

Sharina nodded, her face softening as a gentle smile appeared. "Go. I promise, I will be here for your mate. I will guard her with my life and won't let anyone near her except Fallon, should she happen to come by."

"Thank you, Mama." Trigger gathered his mother into his arms, giving her a tight hug. He knew he was being ridiculous. He was only going to be gone for a brief time, and he would just be down the hall. But he didn't want to leave his mate. His mother understood, and was doing what she could to help him just as she'd always done. "I love you."

"Love you too, baby."

5

Alanna slowly clawed her way out of the dark fog she felt like she was drowning in. She'd spent so much time there lately she was afraid it was going to become permanent, and there was no way she was going to allow that to happen. It was time to wake the hell up and take back her life.

When she finally felt like her head was clear enough to think coherent thoughts, she paused to take stock of how she felt and her surroundings. She was aware of what was happening. It wasn't the first time she'd spent time in that dark and dismal place, and she knew it wouldn't be the last. It happened without fail whenever she used her ability to heal, but this time was different. For the first time that she could remember, her memories of what happened were fragmented. She couldn't recall who she healed, or even why she had to use her gift to heal in the first place. It was all blank. Which was strange. She always remembered who she helped.

The vague recollection of voices teased her mind, one

that was soft and female, and one deep and growly. Unfortunately, she had no idea who they belonged to or why anyone would be around when she was swimming in her pit of hell in the first place. The only person who should have been with her when she was enduring the aftermath of using her abilities was Fallon. And for some reason, she didn't think that female voice was Fallon's that she'd heard.

Letting out a quiet sigh, Alanna began to move, first her hands, and then her feet. It was difficult to do, but not impossible. Her body felt heavy, but it still did what she asked of it, even if it was slow going. That was all right. The only thing that mattered was that she could move, and she wasn't in unbearable agony when she did it. Her entire body ached, but it was manageable. Her head was sore, her chest felt tight, and she felt like her mouth was full of cotton, but at least she wasn't frozen in place, unable to communicate with anyone.

Moaning softly, she licked her dry, chapped lips, and then tried to swallow. She was so thirsty. And hungry. Her stomach felt empty, as if she hadn't eaten in days, which she probably hadn't. She wondered how long she'd been stuck in the darkness this time. It seemed like forever.

Prying her eyes open, Alanna froze when she was able to focus, and her gaze landed on the dark-haired male who sat next to the bed she was laying in. He was huge, way too big for the small chair he sat on. He looked really uncomfortable and utterly exhausted, with his head tilted to the side, eyes closed, and mouth slightly open. He wore a pair of light gray jogging pants with a tight, black t-shirt that was molded to his muscular frame. It appeared as if he'd run his fingers through his hair several times, leaving it with a soft, messy look, and her breath hitched as she wondered what it would feel like to touch the dark strands. Her hand actually twitched where it lay on the bed, and then moved slowly across the light blue comforter in his direction.

Alanna stopped herself when she realized she was reaching for him, wanting to touch him more than she wanted to breathe right then, but she knew she shouldn't. She needed to figure out what the hell was going on. Why was she there? A frown tugged at the corners of her mouth as she realized she didn't know where 'there' was.

"He hasn't left your side except for a few minutes to shower once a day since he brought you home. Not even for meals. I had to bring his food in here or he wouldn't eat."

Alanna's gaze moved to the woman who stood in the doorway, watching her with a soft, warm smile on her face. Her eyes widened when she recognized Trigger's mother. *Shit.*

Well, that answered one of her questions. She was obviously in her mate's house, one he shared with his mother. Alanna should know, because she'd been dropping by and leaving things for Sharina when Chase and Angel sent Trigger out of town on a mission. She knew the woman didn't go outside the small cottage. Ever. She didn't know why and didn't consider it her business. All she cared about was helping the tigress while her son was out of town, and seeing the tiny smiles on her face when she opened the door to see the different presents on her steps each day. A small plant, some cupcakes Alanna had made herself, a stuffed tiger, cookies. So many different little things that made her heart happy when she saw Sharina's face light up with joy.

Sharina crossed the room to stand next to Alanna, reaching out to place a palm on her forehead, and then running the back of her hand softly over Alanna's cheek. Her eyes were filled with tenderness, and that gentle smile was still on her lips. "How are you feeling, sweet daughter?"

Alanna stiffened at the endearment, her eyes widening as her heart began to race. Since when had this woman started to call her daughter? The tigress had to be the female voice she'd remembered, and Trigger the male, but she still couldn't recall much else. A tremor ran through her as she watched Sharina carefully, struggling to remember what happened.

"I can see the confusion in your eyes," Sharina murmured, lifting her hand to run it gently down Alanna's hair. "Do you need some help remembering what happened?"

Alanna bit her lip and nodded, before glancing over at Trigger. He hadn't moved from the position he'd been in, but she knew immediately that he was awake now and paying attention to every word that was being said. There was a slight frown on his brow, and a hint of tension showing in the lines around his eyes. His lips were pressed together where his mouth had just been open a little bit.

Definitely awake.

Her fingers flexed and Alanna found her hand moving toward her mate again. She froze, grasping the sheet with those damn traitorous fingers. When Sharina began speaking, Alanna moved her gaze back to the tigress, but didn't loosen her grip on the sheet. She was afraid if she did she would reach out for her mate and she was still disoriented, unsure how she was there in his house when she'd been avoiding him for so long.

"When my son came home from a mission just over three weeks ago, it was to find that you had just saved the life of Phoenix and Serenity's daughter. In doing so, you almost lost your own. He found you in the hospital, right after you healed the baby. You were in so much pain and had lost consciousness. Doc Josie wanted to put you in a room there and look after you, but Fallon said it wouldn't help. She explained the situation, and Trigger decided to bring you here so we could take care of you and keep you safe."

Over three weeks? Holy cow. She'd never been under that long before.

"Nevaeh," Alanna rasped as the image of the tiny baby with a full head of pitch-black hair surfaced. A small smile tilted up the corners of her lips as she remembered the child's cries when she passed her over to her mother. Proof she was alive and on the mend. When Sharina cocked an eyebrow in question, Alanna managed to whisper, "Their daughter. Nevaeh."

"Ah, so that is the child's name?"

Alanna gave a small nod, closing her eyes when her temples throbbed lightly. She licked at her dry lips again, wishing she had something to drink. Suddenly, there was a spoon at her lips, and she opened them automatically, grateful when she felt the cool water trickle into her mouth. It was perfect. Amazing. And she was quiet for several minutes while someone spoon fed her the water, wiping up any access liquid that dribbled down her chin.

She probably should have been embarrassed that someone was seeing her like this besides Fallon, but she was too tired to think about it.

Finally, when she'd had enough, Alanna forced her eyes open and found herself looking into the deep brown gaze of her mate, the dark green flecks embedded in the brown captivating her. She'd never seen eyes like his before and found that she didn't want to look away.

"You have an IV for fluids, but my son has made sure to keep moisture on your lips so they didn't become dry and chapped," Sharina said, that loving smile back on her lips. "Fallon and I tried to help a few times, but he wanted to take care of you himself."

A memory flashed in her mind and Alanna swallowed hard, her gaze meeting Trigger's as she whispered, "Angry." When his brow furrowed, she tried again, "You were angry." Her arm raised as she lowered her eyes to his mouth and touched the tips of her fingers to his full, lower lip. "Fangs."

Trigger caught her hand in his and placed a kiss on the tip of her fingers as her eyes closed against her will. She couldn't seem to hold a conversation. For some reason, it was harder to talk than it normally was when she recovered from healing someone. Probably because she was so close to death claiming her this time. She was also so damn tired. Just exhausted. She needed to sleep for a couple of days straight. A real sleep, not one where she was stuck in darkness and terrified she would never find her way out.

Alanna was aware of Sharina slipping out of the room and quietly closing the door behind her, but when she finally managed to open her eyes again, she couldn't tear her gaze away from Trigger's.

Her mind raced with so many questions. How long had he known they were mates? Had he been avoiding her when she was hiding from him? Better yet, did he know she'd been hiding from him?

And the big question. Did he want her? Did he want to tie their souls together for life? Did she want that? She couldn't have that, could she? Not when her life expectancy had somehow dwindled down to just a few more short months recently.

"Yes," he said gruffly, "I was pissed the fuck off." When she lifted her brows, his gaze darkened. "They took advantage of you when I wasn't here to protect you, mate. They had you heal the child knowing she was dying. Knowing you could have died." She watched entranced as those fangs she'd just mentioned made an appearance and a shudder ran through his big body. "You are mine to protect. Mine to keep safe. I could have lost you before I even had a chance to claim you, Alanna."

Alanna heard the rage in his voice. The fury at the thought that others had put her in danger and risked her life. But that wasn't the case. Not really. Granted, Phoenix had come for her and requested her help, but no one made her do anything. She made the decision herself, and she did it because it was the right thing to do. She wouldn't change it if she could, not even for the man in front of her.

"My fault," she whispered, unable to turn away from the raw, turbulent emotion on his face. She knew he was angry with everyone right now because in his mind they didn't protect her, but he needed to understand that there was nothing they could have done. She would have healed Nevaeh no matter what. "My choice. Not theirs."

Trigger's gaze darkened even more if that were possible. "Did they or did they not ask you to heal the baby, Alanna?" When she bit her lip and dropped her gaze from the barely banked rage in his eyes that he didn't even try to conceal, Trigger placed the cup of water on the nightstand, and sat on the edge of the bed. Cupping her cheek in his large hand, he leaned over and placed a soft kiss on her forehead. "I'm not mad at you, sweet mate. I am furious with Phoenix for asking what he did of you. And with Chase, Angel, and Josie for allowing it to happen. But no part of me is mad at you."

"Had to save her," Alanna rasped. "Just a baby. Deserves a chance at life."

"So do you," Trigger growled, as he rubbed the pad of his thumb over her skin where he still cradled her jaw, causing a shiver of desire to run down her spine. Alanna froze in shock as she realized she was excited for his touch, wanted to feel his hands stroking over her body, even in the state she was in right now. If he could scent her arousal, he didn't let it show. He just continued on with the discussion. "I will tell you exactly what I told all of them, Alanna. Your life is just as precious as Phoenix and Serenity's daughter's is. Trying to exchange your life for hers is not acceptable." He held up a hand when she would have interrupted. "I didn't want anything to happen to her either, sweetheart. I'm not a monster, and she is an innocent child. But I hate the fact that everyone was willing to let you die so another could live. No matter who it is, whose life is in jeopardy, I can't get behind that. I just can't."

"One of the Gods spoke to me," Alanna whispered, trying to make him understand. "When I was healing her. Said Nevaeh's special. She needs to live. Will be important to the pack one day."

Lowering his head, he rested his forehead against hers. "*You* are important too, my mate. You are not just a healer. *You* matter. To me. I will fight for you while you fight for others, if I have to. I will do whatever I need to — put myself between you and the world to make sure you live."

Alanna fought back tears as she closed her eyes and leaned into his touch. She'd never had anyone care so much for her before. No one had stood between her and the cruelty life had thrown at her. No one had challenged her brother or his friends when they beat her, punished her for things she had no control over, and just plain treated her like dirt. Here was a man who looked like he was willing to take on the world for her. To fight all her demons. Could she accept that? Accept him? She wanted to let him in more than anything, but what about the boy who needed her? Who would die without her help? Could she be selfish and place herself first for once?

She knew that answer before she even asked herself the question. No, she could never put her life ahead of a child's. She would be there for that little boy when it was time because he needed her. She couldn't turn her back on him no matter what.

That being said, she was going to have to figure something out and quick. Because while she would never put her life in front of any child's, she refused to deny her mate anymore. He was wonderful. One of the most amazing people she'd ever met. He had taken care of her when she was going through one of her episodes, never leaving her side from what his mother said. He was her dark knight, willing to take on the world for her, if she let him.

She wanted to.

She wanted him.

Needed him.

She was done fighting it.

As she let her eyes close, she let the one word slip out that she'd been wanting to say ever since she woke and found him beside her. "Mine."

She was unaware of the slow grin that crossed Trigger's face as he slowly traced his fingers over her cheek and down the side of her neck to the place where he would place his mark when they claimed each other.

"Mine." His deep voice rang with stark satisfaction and a need that would have set her body on fire, if she wasn't utterly exhausted.

Alanna let the world fade away as she finally lost consciousness, slipping into a deep healing sleep.

6

Trigger stood in the shower, one hand on the wall just under and to the right of the showerhead, his head bowed as the water rained down on him. He had it as hot as he could stand it in hopes it would help clear some of the cobwebs from his head. He was so fucking tired.

It had been weeks since he'd gotten any real rest, and the past couple of days watching Alanna as she slept had been even worse. He had hardly closed his eyes at all. Fortunately, he could tell that this time it was a different kind of sleep than what she'd been in before. It was the only thing that was keeping him sane, because unlike when she'd at least opened her pretty brown eyes every once in a while, this time there had been no movement at all out of her. None. He wouldn't even know she was alive if it wasn't for the steady beat of her heart and the breath flowing through her lungs, which he found himself checking constantly.

Then there was the ache in his cock that was driving

him crazy. He'd been rock hard ever since the tantalizing scent of his mate's arousal filled the air when she'd last been awake. He'd managed to somehow ignore it at the time, knowing there was no way she could do anything about it, but since then he'd been in hell.

His mom was in the guest bedroom down the hall with Alanna, and he was stuck in the damn shower with his cock so hard he could pound fucking nails with it while he fought the urge to stroke himself off. It felt wrong to do something like that when his mate was so close, but if he waited too much longer, he was going to have a serious case of blue balls.

Trigger stifled a groan, his hand going to his dick. He wrapped his fingers tightly around it, squeezing to try and push back the orgasm that wanted to break free. It was ridiculous, but he didn't want to go there without Alanna. For some reason, just the idea of it swamped him with guilt.

Loosen your hold, my tiger.

Trigger froze as the sound of his mate's voice slid into his head. His heart began to pound, matching the beat of the pulse in his cock.

He frowned. Was it really her, or was he seriously going crazy right now? He knew all the members of RARE, Angel's team of mercenaries, had the gift of telepathy, but he personally had no psychic abilities whatsoever. Alanna had the ability to heal; did she have other gifts he wasn't aware of? Could she really talk to him like this?

It's me, mate. The sound of her voice speaking so intimately in his mind nearly drove him wild as his hand tightened even more around his cock in the hopes that he wouldn't accidentally come right then and there. He heard soft laughter, and then, *Isn't that the idea? To come?*

Don't want to without you, he grumbled, hoping she could hear him the way he could hear her.

Holy shit, was this really happening? Or was he dreaming?

Oh, it's happening, mate. Just stay quiet and enjoy the experience.

Trigger's eyes sprang open wide when he felt the light touch of fingers ghosting down his chest. He snarled, baring his teeth, but didn't move.

Sshhh, it's just me.

How the hell are you doing that?

Her hands trailed lower, stopping just above where he was gripping his shaft like it was a damn lifeline. She chuckled, and then lowered one of her hands down to cradle his balls, rolling them gently.

Don't worry about that right now. Move your hand, cat. I want to play. I know you want to wait for me, but I want to do this for you. I need *to. Please.*

Trigger groaned low and deep as he let go of his dick and braced his forearms against the shower wall, resting his forehead on them. Giving in to something he didn't completely understand but didn't have the will to fight, he rasped, *Baby, please, work your magic. I hurt.*

Another groan slipped out when he felt her fingers slowly whisper over his aching cock, sliding up one side and then down the other before her small hand wrapped around him in a firm grip.

"Fuck," he muttered, his body shaking as she began moving one hand up and down his length while tugging lightly on his balls with the other. He cursed silently when he felt her tongue lick over one of his nipples before she bit down lightly on it, and then sucked it into her mouth.

I have no idea how the hell you are doing what you are doing, but it feels so fucking good, baby.

Alanna moved over to his other nipple, sucking on it as her grip on him tightened, her hand moving faster. She slid her thumb over the tip, coating it with his pre-cum and smearing it over the top of his cock before sliding her hand back down to the base. His breathing became harsher and faster as he felt her lips skim down his chest to his straining cock, and then her tongue licked over the top of it and she sucked just the tip into her mouth. He was so far gone that was all it took.

He shoved his face into his arms, muffling his shout of satisfaction as he came hard, coating the wall in front of him with strips of white. His body shook with pleasure, his heart thundering in his chest as he whispered, *Thank you, my sweet mate. Soon, I'll return the favor, with my face between your legs, and my tongue licking up all your delicious honey.*

Finish your shower, cat. You can show me all your amazing skills later when your mom isn't looking at me like she really wants to ask a question but isn't sure she should as her nostrils are flaring.

Trigger chuckled, shaking his head at his mate's antics. He paused, a wide smile spreading across his face as he realized that Alanna had just shown him a side of herself that he'd never seen before. She was sassy, sensual, confident. And the way her laughter had flitted through his head, it teased his senses, making him want more. More of everything.

Seeing this new side of her suddenly made two things

clear to him. One, she was finally feeling better after everything she'd endured. Maybe not a hundred percent, but a lot better than she had been over the last few weeks. And two, unless he was mistaken, she was ready to stop running from him and complete their bond. The thought of that sent another rush of desire through him that had his cock standing to attention again.

Ignoring it, Trigger got out of the shower and quickly started to dry off. He wanted to see his woman. He needed to check on her, hear her beautiful voice again, and see for himself that she was feeling better. Because if she was, he was ready to have a talk that had been a long time coming. One that would make her his for the rest of their lives.

7

Alanna slowly pushed herself up into a sitting position, her eyes on the woman who was now standing on the other side of the room facing the window. She knew her face was flushed with desire and embarrassment and the scent of both was heavy in the room. Thankfully, Sharina wasn't looking at her now, giving her a chance to get control of her emotions.

She couldn't believe she'd just helped Trigger... do what she did... while his mother was in the room with her. Or even that she'd done it at all. She wasn't experienced in the sex department. She'd never done anything like that before. The extent of her sexual activity came from things she'd read in romance novels or watched on television.

No one in her sleuth was ever brave enough to show interest in her because of her brother. He would have killed them. And she was never on her own except for when she was waitressing. It wasn't allowed. Doug kept a close eye on her because in his mind she belonged to him.

She wasn't anything more than a slave, and he refused to give her up for any reason.

"Trigger's father and I weren't fated mates."

Alanna's eyes widened in surprise at the quietly spoken words, and she paused in the act of trying to scoot back to sit against the wooden headboard. Her gaze met Sharina's when the tigress turned from the window to look at her, and she had to stifle a gasp at the anguish she saw in her beautiful amber eyes.

Sharina walked over to Alanna and grabbed two pillows, fluffing them up and setting them against the headboard, and then she helped her move back against them.

"Comfortable?"

Alanna nodded, giving the woman a genuine affectionate smile. "Yes. Thank you, Sharina."

She watched as Sharina lowered herself into the chair next to the bed, wondering again about her comment before. She'd wondered about Trigger's father, who and where he was, but she was ashamed that it had been no more than a fleeting thought. She'd been more interested in his mother, and the relationship between the two of them.

All the thoughts running through her mind fled when Sharina reached out and grasped her hand, and Alanna was suddenly flooded with so many different emotions it was hard for her to distinguish them all. She was an empath, and while it wasn't one of her strongest abilities, the touch of someone who was experiencing deep feelings could cause her gift to flare, intensifying all of the emotions when Alanna was hit with them. She was normally able to somewhat block them, but Sharina's had taken her by surprise and all she could do was feel.

Deep depressing sorrow. Rage that could burn an entire city to the ground if it ever combusted. Fear. Anxiousness and apprehension that was almost debilitating. But the strongest was love and a fierce determination, which seemed to be the only thing holding the others back from taking over and consuming the poor woman's life.

"What was his name?" Alanna asked softly, wanting to know more about Trigger and his family, but also wanting to somehow help the woman who meant so much to her mate if she could.

Sharina gave her a tremulous smile, her eyes misting over with tears. "William. We grew up together. Best friends since the first day we met. He stole my heart, and I never looked back. We married in our early twenties, even though we both knew we could have fated mates out there somewhere in the world. We just loved each other so much."

Alanna was aware of Trigger now standing in the doorway, but she didn't take her eyes from his mother. "I think that sounds beautiful. I can't imagine how it feels to love someone like that and to have them return your love. It must have been the most amazing feeling in the world."

Sharina bit her lip, glancing down at their hands. "You don't think it was wrong? Forsaking our mates the way we did?"

Alanna cocked her head to the side, looking at the tigress closely. Guilt was foremost in Sharina's emotions now and she didn't like that. In her opinion, this kind, giving woman had nothing to feel guilty about. "Love is never wrong, Sharina. I believe the Gods put William in your life for a reason. You had a wonderful life together, and he gave you a son to cherish. One who loves you unconditionally and would do anything for you. I see nothing wrong with any of that."

The grip on her hand tightened and tears began to trickle down Sharina's cheeks. "Our parents didn't want us to get married. They said it was selfish of us and we should wait for our true mates. That if we found them, we wouldn't be able to stay away from them and it would ruin the life we were trying to build together."

Alanna thought about that for a moment before she replied. "There is a pull between mates that is hard to deny. It's strong and becomes stronger day by day. While I agree with your parents in the aspect that you wouldn't have been able to stay away from your true mates, I still say love is never wrong. You and William wanting to spend as much of your lives together as possible was a beautiful thing, not something that was wrong. Who's to say you would have ever found your mates? Then you would have lived your lives alone, without love, and without a son who completed your family."

A short sob escaped and Sharina whispered, "That's exactly how we felt. We wanted to love and care for each other for as long as we could, no matter what the future held." Sharina's eyes met hers, and the feeling of guilt turned to one of extreme sadness. "The day I lost my William was one I will never forget. They came out of the trees; an army it seemed like. Humans who knew about shifters and thought they all needed to be extinguished." She paused, then took a deep breath before she continued. "My people fought hard, but there were just too many of them. They slaughtered everyone they saw, man, woman, and child. It didn't matter. Even the human mates in our streak were killed. It was a blood bath. Something I will never forget."

As Sharina spoke, Alanna began to do something she had never tried before. She was a healer to her core, and she couldn't just sit by and let Trigger's mother drown in her emotions. By the look and feel of it, she'd been doing it for far too long. She was practically suffocating from it all.

Concentrating on the sorrow that was cloaked around the tigress, Alanna began to push her healing power toward it. Praying she could at least lessen it, along with some of the other stronger emotions, so Sharina could breathe normally again.

"My husband fought hard with Trigger by his side, but when it became obvious who the victors would be, he made Trigger take me and run. I didn't want to go. If William was going to die, I wanted to take the same path he was on. I didn't want to live without him." Her eyes seemed to beg for Alanna's understanding. "I know I should have wanted to live for my son. William wasn't my mate, there was no mate bond, but the pull to be with him..."

"It is my belief that the pull of love can be almost as strong as the pull of a mate bond."

"Really?" Sharina whispered, more tears slipping out and down her face.

"Really," Alanna promised. "While it might be something I've never experienced myself, it is something I firmly believe. I've felt it between humans I've met before. An undying love. One that seemed to be similar to the bond between mates." Alanna reached out and cradled the other woman's face in her hand as she pushed more and more healing power her way. "You need to let the guilt go, Sharina. You wanted to stay with the man you love. It didn't mean you loved your son any less. I've seen how much you care for him, and he knows it too. All the sorrow, the rage you are feeling, it isn't good to hold onto it the way you are. It's crushing you."

"I'm so mad at the humans who murdered my family, my friends, my streak. So furious," Sharina snarled. "And the pain of losing all of them, how do I let that go, Alanna? How? It's been so long and I can't seem to forget."

"You don't forget, Mama," Alanna whispered, smiling when Sharina's breath hitched at the title she used. "You concentrate on the good times. All of the love you shared. The happiness you felt. And you give everything else to me."

Alanna tugged on the hand that was still clasped tightly with hers. Moving over slightly, she pulled Sharina up next to her on the bed. The tigress slid down, laid her head in Alanna's lap and cried huge racking sobs that pulled at Alanna's heart and caused her own tears to slip free.

"That's it," Alanna murmured, as she ran her hand over Sharina's hair. "I've got you, Mama." She held Trigger's mother, the new mother of her heart. She spoke gently to her, words of love and acceptance, as she began to pull all the guilt, anger, and sadness from the tormented woman, bringing it into her own body, absorbing it the way she would if she were healing a wound. The pain and suffering would become hers to bear for the next few days and she welcomed it. Even though she'd just gone through hell after saving Nevaeh, she refused to let her mate's mother go through her misery any longer.

Even after Sharina fell asleep, exhaustion claiming her, Alanna continued to stroke a calming hand down her hair, absorbing every negative emotion she could until she was satisfied she'd removed it all. When she finally allowed herself to break free, she leaned her head back and closed her eyes.

After a long moment, she felt Trigger's presence next to her, and she slowly turned her head to look at him. His eyes were filled with worry and wet with unshed tears. Giving him a small, tired smile, Alanna whispered, "She's going to be okay. I promise."

"What about you?" he asked quietly.

Alanna's smile widened and she gave a small shrug. "I honestly don't know. I've never done anything like that before." At his confused look, she said, "I've healed physical injuries, but I've never tried to heal emotions before. I didn't know it was something I could even do. I have no idea what it will do to me, but whatever happens, I will gladly take it on for a few days if it means your mother will be free of it for the rest of her life."

"Fuck," Trigger growled lowly, scrubbing a hand over his face. "I shouldn't have let you do that. I didn't know exactly what was happening, but it was obvious something was. I should have said something. Should have protected you. Hell, I'm no better than Phoenix and the rest of them."

Alanna couldn't stand the self-loathing in his voice. If they were going to give this a try, he was going to need to change his way of thinking. While she loved how protective he was of her, she refused to stop living her life the way she believed she needed to, no matter what happened. It was her calling to heal, and she wouldn't turn away from it.

"You can't stop me from healing others, my tiger," she said quietly. When a dark look appeared in his eyes, she held up a hand, wincing when the needle hooked to the IV tugged on her skin. "Please, Trigger, listen to me. What I do, it's a calling to me. It isn't something I can turn off. I believe I was put on this earth to help others, that it is what the Gods want of me. And it's something I *want* to do."

"It's going to get you killed someday," he snarled. "What the hell kind of mate would I be if I let that happen?"

"The kind I need by my side," she said bluntly, knowing it was going to just piss him off more.

"What the fuck?"

"I can't stand by and watch people suffer if I can help them, Trigger. I *save* lives. I make a difference. Can't you see how much it means to me that your mother will be free of all the sadness and despair she's had since your father was taken from you? How happy I am that I could remove the rage that is always simmering just below the surface because your entire family and streak were murdered? She will be able to build a new life now, one filled with love and laughter. And maybe, just maybe, she will find a mate someday. One that will make her feel as protected and cherished as you've made me feel these past few weeks."

Trigger's gaze went to his mother, where Alanna was still running her hand gently down Sharina's long curls. She was sleeping peacefully now, her face a picture of calm serenity. Her lips curved up into a hint of a small smile.

"And the joy I feel at knowing little Nevaeh has a chance at life now. That she will grow into a courageous woman who will be very important to the pack. Not to mention how happy it made me that I could free the alpha from what pain he was still feeling when he was shot protecting Jinx. He saved me from my brother, Trigger, and I got to return the favor. And poor Raven. She was hurting so much after her ordeal. I was able to give her a pain free life. One she wouldn't have had if I wasn't blessed with the gifts I have."

"And if you die following this calling?" Trigger ground out, his eyes flashing, his cat near the surface.

"Then I die, but I will go knowing I saved a life."

"If you died, no matter the reason, mate, I would follow."

He would, too. It was written all over his face. She hated it, but she knew there was no way she would want to live without him if he were to lose his life on one of his missions. Now that she'd fully accepted him, there was no other outcome if something were to happen to either of them.

Alanna held out a hand to the man she was losing her heart to, letting out a breath she didn't realize she was holding when he captured it with his own. "Same, mate."

Trigger sat in silence for a long moment, his dark eyes never leaving hers. "Exactly how many different abilities do you have, Alanna?"

She could tell by the look on his face that there was a reason he was asking, but she answered him truthfully, because she would never lie to him. "Four, possibly five, but I haven't tried to hone the fifth one, since I have no desire to talk to the dead." When he raised an eyebrow, she shrugged. "You know of my healing ability. I'm also an empath, which means I can feel the emotions of others. It isn't a strong gift of mine. I have to actually touch someone, or their feelings have to be really strong before I connect with them. Telepathy is another one, which you know from earlier." She grinned at the hot, molten look that entered his eyes. "I wish I could use that one when I'm under after healing someone, but I can't. I can't actually use any of my gifts. I'm in too much pain and am just plain exhausted. I also have visions. They are almost always about the future, but I can't ever really pinpoint the time they will take place. I just know it is going to happen."

Trigger nodded, his eyes never leaving hers when he asked, "So, which one of them is the one that kept you away from me all these months?"

She stiffened, shock filling her at the assumption he'd come to during their discussion. The very accurate deduction. Which brought to mind another question. "How long have you known?"

"It took me a while to figure it out. I would catch faint traces of your scent, but I didn't realize what it was exactly. It wasn't until I saw you leave Raven's hospital room a couple of months ago that it all fell into place. I would have said something then, but you seemed distracted and left quickly. Before I could follow you, I heard the people with Raven talking about how you helped her, and I needed a little time to come to grips with everything. By the time I did, we were already deep into the dance of you avoiding me, and I thought it would be best to give you some space until you were ready."

Alanna glanced down at the bed, took a deep breath, and then met his gaze again. "To be honest, I wasn't planning on ever saying anything." When deep growls began in Trigger's chest at her confession, Alanna rushed on, "Trust me, it wasn't because I didn't want to. I did; so much. I practically stalked you. I couldn't stay away. I watched you around the compound." She hesitated before admitting, "Someone told me about your mom never leaving the house. And how when you were away on missions she was always alone. I didn't like the thought of that, so I started bringing things when I knew you were gone."

"That was you?" Trigger whispered.

She raised her head and nodded. "I hated that she was alone, afraid to leave the house, but I also did it for you since you weren't here to do it yourself." She shrugged. "It made her happy, which made me happy. I never had a mother who loved me like yours does you. Mine didn't really want anything to do with me. Neither did my father or anyone else."

"Are you telling me that no one has ever shown you love before, little bear?"

"Fallon is my best friend, and I don't know what I would do without her. She shows me how much she cares for me, but not even she has ever told me she loves me," Alanna admitted, her eyes dropping down to where Sharina lay in her lap. "I've seen love before though. I know what it is. It just isn't something I've ever had for myself."

Trigger leaned over, rubbing her cheek with his. "You deserve to be loved, sweet mate."

Alanna soaked in the warmth and caring she could feel coming from him, before she finally told him the truth in a soft whisper. "I had a vision. Someone is coming for me. I don't know when, but when he does I will go with him because there is no other choice. If I don't, a little boy will die." When Trigger stiffened but stayed silent, she said, "This may be something I don't walk away from. I've seen nothing in the future for myself after I heal him. Nothing at all. So, I stayed away because I thought it would be better if you didn't know about me in case I don't make it back. I didn't want you to hurt, to mourn a dead mate. I… I thought it would be better to never know you had one than to be put through something like that."

Trigger's breathing had become harsher, the hand on hers tightening to an almost punishing grip. "You will go help this boy, knowing you may not survive?"

"Yes," she whispered, rubbing her cheek against his as tears streamed down her face. "Yes, I will."

Trigger rose and took a step back. He looked at her, his face a cold, blank mask before he turned and walked out of the bedroom. She sat in stunned silence as the front door slammed. A few minutes later a loud roar echoed throughout the area, followed by another, and another. They started out sounding full of fury but ended in anguish as the sounds led far away from her until there was nothing.

8

Trigger raced across the ground as fast as his tiger could go, weaving in and out of the forest of trees and leaping over anything in his path. He'd been shot before. Tortured for two days straight in the military after being captured by the enemy. Lost his father, family, and streak. None of the pain he'd felt from any of those things was remotely close to the agony that he was experiencing now. It felt as if it was ripping his chest wide open, squeezing his heart so tightly it was about to burst.

He was going to lose her. The one person who was meant to be the other half of his soul. The woman he was supposed to spend the rest of his life caring for, loving, and protecting. He was going to lose her because of a gift that seemed to mean more to her than a lifetime with him.

As the last thought rolled through his mind, Trigger began to slow his strides until he was standing still. His head hung low to the ground, his sides heaving with every breath he took. As he stood there, shame began to fill him as he remembered the conversation he'd had with his mate while she'd been holding his beautiful mama in his lap. *After* Alanna had done everything she could to help end the heartache and suffering his mother had endured ever since their streak was attacked.

She'd saved Nevaeh, willing to give her life for the child's because she saw it as her calling. A gift she said was given to her by the Gods to help others. But Trigger knew it was more than that. She may believe it was her calling, but she'd also done it for Phoenix and Serenity, members of her new pack who she cared deeply for. And for the baby who deserved a chance to live and experience the joys life had to offer.

As angry as it made him that his mate thought it was okay to exchange her life for someone else's, Trigger knew he would do the exact same thing if it was him. If he had Alanna's ability to heal, he wouldn't hesitate to do whatever it took to save any person in his pack. He would give his life for theirs in a heartbeat. Just as he would for any child, pack or not.

Which brought forth the question, why did he think it was okay if he did it but not Alanna?

Throwing his head back, Trigger let out a loud, agony-filled roar before lowering his huge body to the ground and resting his head on his paws. That question was easy to answer. Because she was *his* dammit. He was supposed to protect her. It was his duty and his right.

He wanted to be the one to show his mate what love was. To shower her with the emotion that she'd been denied all of her life, and hopefully have those feelings returned. It had been a long time since anyone had loved him besides his mother, and he wanted to know what it was like to feel that emotion from Alanna. Trigger bet it would be amazing to be loved by someone like her. A woman who was sweet, kind, and generous. One so selfless and giving.

He huffed, raising his large head and giving it a shake of frustration. If anyone was selfish, it was him. Alanna gave of herself to everyone, no matter the cost, because she had a heart bigger than anyone he knew, and here he was upset and wallowing in self-pity, thinking her gift meant more to her than he did. His sweet bear had stayed away, knowing if she allowed him to claim her it would kill him if he lost her. She'd tried to save him, once again looking out for someone besides herself and what she needed.

Well, that was going to stop right now. It was his job as her mate to take care of her and keep her safe, and that was what he was going to do. Healing others was important to her, and as much as he hated how it put her in danger, he understood why she would want to do it. If she was insistent on using the ability, then he was damn well going to support her and figure out a way to protect her in the aftermath.

Slowly, Trigger rose to his feet, stretching his legs out one at a time before he turned and headed back home at a fast clip. He wasn't sure how long he'd been gone, but knew it was at least two if not more hours, and he needed to check on his mate. He'd just walked out and left her like a fucking prick. He needed to make sure she was okay, and then he wanted to talk to his alpha. He needed… no, *they* needed help.

The first thing Trigger saw when the pale green cottage came into view was Doc Josie's car sitting out front. He was around to the back of the house, shifted and dressed, and walking in the back door within five minutes. He entered to the sound of female laughter and stopped at the sight in front of him.

His mother, Alanna, and the doc sat at the kitchen table, each with a cup of coffee and a handful of homemade chocolate chip cookies in front of them. He could see that Alanna was free of the IV, feeding tube, and catheter, and looked as if she'd not only taken a shower but had shifted at least once while he was gone, making her appear almost as if the past few weeks had never happened.

The women paused in their discussion and looked over at him, the room becoming almost uncomfortably quiet and still.

Trigger couldn't tear his gaze from his mate. She made his heart pound erratically. Her gorgeous, long brown hair lay over her shoulders and down her back. He knew it was just as thick and soft as it looked, and he wanted to slide his fingers through it again. She'd just been laughing, but her big brown eyes held no humor. He couldn't scent any real joy or happiness from her, no matter what the smile on her face said. His eyes dropped to her lips that were a beautiful shade of pink to see the full bottom one was trembling. Something was wrong.

Crossing the room to her, he squatted down and leaned over to place a gentle kiss on her forehead, then the tip of her nose, following up with a light one on her soft lips. When she sucked in a breath, he had to force himself to pull away so he didn't lengthen the kiss into something not appropriate in his kitchen right now.

"You doing okay, sweet mate?"

Alanna's smile widened, but it still didn't reach her eyes. Instead of replying, she gave him a small nod that had him even more suspicious. Either she was upset with him for taking off the way he did, or it was something else.

Narrowing his eyes, he said, "Sorry I left earlier. I needed to get away. To take a run so I could think things through."

"That's okay," she replied softly. "I understand."

It was an honest answer. There was no scent of a lie.

Raising a hand, he placed a finger on her temple and tapped it twice, hoping she would understand what he wanted. She bit her bottom lip and glanced over to his mother, before leaning in and placing her forehead on his shoulder.

I don't want her to know.

Know what, sweetheart?

At first, he wasn't sure she was going to respond, but then he heard, *The way taking her emotions from her is affecting me.*

Shit. What exactly did that mean?

Trigger placed a hand on the back of Alanna's neck and held her to him as he glanced over at his mother and Josie. "How are things going, Doc?" He didn't know what else to say. Their last meeting hadn't gone so well.

It's okay, Alanna. Let them talk for a minute or two and I will get you back to the bedroom so you can rest.

"Things are okay."

He heard the distance in Josie's voice and he didn't blame her. He'd been harsh with her the last time they'd seen each other and all she'd been trying to do was help. He'd been lucky her mate, Ryker, hadn't paid him a visit afterwards. He would have deserved it. "Look, Doc, I want to apologize for the way I treated you before."

"It's okay," Josie said quietly. "If I were in your shoes, I probably would have felt the same way."

"No, it's not okay. I was wrong." When her eyes rounded in surprise, he sighed. "I came home after an intense mission to find my mate near death's door, Doc. I kind of lost it. Alanna and I hadn't even acknowledged each other as mates yet, and all I could think about was how I might lose her before I'd even had a chance to claim her. I took it out on all of you. I shouldn't have."

Josie shook her head, her eyes filling with tears. "No, you were right to defend Alanna, Trigger. We shouldn't have put her in the situation we did."

Trigger stood and helped Alanna to her feet beside him, tucking her into his side. Leaning down to brush a kiss over the top of her head, he said, "My mate was right where she was needed at the time, Doc." Alanna's gaze shot up to his and she gasped in surprise. "You spoke and I listened, sweetheart. It just took me a little bit of time to wrap my mind around it all. You were put on this earth to help people. To save lives. And I am so fucking proud of you."

Tears gathered in Alanna's eyes and spilled over down her cheeks. This time the smile she gave him was radiant, and full of what could only be classified as love. His little bear may not have said the words yet, but she loved him.

"Thank you." The words were a whisper, so soft he almost didn't hear them.

"You don't ever have to thank me for something like this, little bear. It's something any good mate should do, and I want to be the best mate for you." He placed another kiss to those lips that he wanted to devour, forcing himself to pull back quickly. "I need to go talk to the Alpha. How about I help you back to bed before I go so you can get some rest? I shouldn't be gone long, and we can watch a movie or something when I get back."

"Can I go with you?" Alanna asked tentatively, her chocolate-colored eyes wide with nervousness and something else. Hope?

"To see Chase?"

"Yes, please. I want to be with you, if that's okay."

A wide smile crossed his face, warmth spreading through his chest, and Trigger nodded. "I'd like that."

9

Alanna held Trigger's hand tightly as they entered the building where his team had their meetings. Chase wasn't in his office when they got there, and they'd been directed to this building instead. For some reason she was nervous to see everyone. Nervous to even be out in the open. She didn't know why. Her mate was with her. There wasn't a doubt in her mind that he would keep her safe.

"Talk to me, Alanna."

She glanced around and realized they'd stopped just inside the entrance. She had no idea how long they'd been standing there while she was lost in anxiety that was threatening to consume her.

Trigger wrapped an arm around her waist and pulled her close, her front to his. He rubbed a hand up and down her back while he nuzzled her cheek with his own. She let out a shocked gasp when she felt his lips trail lightly over her skin, down her neck, and over her shoulder. It felt so good, and she found herself tilting her head to the side to give him better access, hoping for more.

"In my mind if you need to, sweet mate, but I won't move from here until I know what's wrong."

Alanna clutched at the front of his shirt, not sure how to explain what she was feeling. She had her suspicions, but she really didn't know if they were true. She'd never experienced anything like what she was going through before.

Taking him at his word, she reached out the only way she could speak at that moment. *I don't know for sure, but I think it has something to do with what happened earlier. With Mama.*

I love it when you call her that. His voice was soft, like a gentle caress, and it made her heart flutter.

It's how I think of her, she admitted. *How I've thought of her since the first time I saw you with her. I wanted her to be my mother too.*

That's good, because she's already claimed you as a daughter.

She heard the amusement in his voice and it helped her relax.

She was filled with so much sadness and rage, but also an almost crippling anxiety. I think that is why she never leaves the house. Because of that anxiety.

Did you take all of those emotions of hers on, like you do when you take people's pain and heal them? Do you think it might be a similar situation? You might not be in pain, but are you having issues controlling your feelings and emotions?

Alanna pushed closer to him, if that were even possible, and nodded. *Yes, I think that's exactly what happened.*

But it's strange, because while I am feeling some of every emotion I pulled from her, it isn't as bad as when I take someone's pain. This is less intense. It's kind of like the majority of it has already bled off and I am just feeling the afterthoughts of it. What I am going through right now is hard, but it's nothing compared to what your mom was feeling.

Trigger slid his hand up her back, through her thick mass of hair, and cupped the back of her head. *Do you think this is as bad as it will get?*

There's no way of knowing, she said honestly, *but I hope so.*

His fingers curled into her long brunette strands and he tugged lightly, tilting her head back so she was staring up at him. *Me too, baby, but let me know right away if it gets worse so I can get you home and take care of you.*

You aren't mad?

He shook his head, leaning down until his lips hovered over hers. *No, sweet mate. I thought a lot about everything when I was out running. It's why I was gone for so long. I had to get my head on straight before I came home to you. I realize your calling to heal is very important to you. I'm not going to take that from you. Instead, I am going to help you in any way possible. I'm going to be here for you to lean on, and I will do everything in my power to keep you safe, but I won't hold you back.*

Alanna let out a small moan when Trigger lowered his head and brushed his lips back and forth over hers. Reaching up, she wrapped her arms around his neck and sank into him. She began to tremble when she felt his tongue skate over her bottom lip, and she opened when he slid past her lips and into her mouth. Her pulse raced as he found her tongue with his and stroked against it again and again.

Sooner than she wanted, Trigger pulled back, smiling down at her. "You taste delicious."

She giggled, ducking her head shyly. "I've never done that before."

He hooked a finger under her chin and raised her head to look at him. His eyes were narrowed on her, and a shiver of awareness ran through her at the heat in them. "Never done what, Alanna?"

She was sure her face was a fiery red when she replied. "Never kissed anyone."

Trigger froze, his mouth opening slightly as his eyebrows rose. "Never?"

She shook her head slowly.

"But what about what we did in the shower?"

Her face couldn't get any redder, could it? "I've read things like that in books before, but never done them myself."

"Oh fuck." Trigger rested his forehead against hers as he growled, "The things you do to me, baby." Stepping back, he tangled his fingers with hers and shook his head. "Let's get this over with. If at any time you feel like you need to get out of there, you say something, okay?" She watched as he tapped his temple twice, and then reached over to hers and did the same thing. "Anytime you need something, I'm here."

She nodded, and then stretched up on the tips of her toes and kissed his lips quickly. "Got it."

Alanna followed Trigger down a long hall, clutching tightly to his hand, her wide gaze going to each room. She'd been in the building once before, but it was months ago. The day after she and Fallon were rescued and the council and Angel were deciding her fate. She'd already known this pack was where she was needed. She'd just needed their approval, which they'd given easily to Angel as Chase's alpha mate.

That same day she met the man who could possibly cause her demise. Yes, she knew who would be coming for her, and she somewhat knew why. She just didn't know when.

Alanna paused just inside the doorway of a room filled with people as a thought came to her. She'd already told Trigger someone would be coming for her. Should she have told him she knew who it was? It wouldn't change the outcome… or would it? She'd never tried to alter her visions before, always assuming the final outcome would be the same. But what if she was wrong? What if the visions could be changed?

"Alanna! It's so good to see you!"

Alanna glanced over to see Angel headed in her direction, her arms outstretched for a hug. She burrowed into Trigger's side, her entire body trembling. She did not want that hug right now. The only one she wanted touching her was Trigger. She knew it was a result of all of his mother's leftover emotions, but she couldn't help how she felt.

Please don't let anyone else touch me, Trigger. I can't. I just can't.

I've got you, my mate.

Stepping in front of her, Trigger held up a hand to stop Angel.

"Dammit Trigger, I just want to talk to her."

"I get it, Angel. I do. But I would appreciate it if you

would please respect her wishes right now and keep it to just talking."

"What?"

"No hugs, okay? No touching at all. Just talking."

"She doesn't want me to touch her?"

Alanna felt horrible when she heard the hurt in Angel's voice. She tried to step around Trigger to get to her, but he slid an arm around her waist and tugged her tightly against him.

"Stop, little bear. I promised you I would always protect you and I will. You have a bad habit of putting everyone else's needs before your own. That stops now. Understand?"

Alanna looked up into his dark brown eyes, feeling that sensation in her heart again. The fluttering one, as if it were going to grow wings and fly. Raising her arm, she ran her hand over his chest, and then grasped his shirt in her fist. Her gaze locked with his, she whispered *Thank you* into his mind.

Do you mind if I share what happened earlier, so she knows why you need this?

Alanna lowered her gaze and slowly ran it around the room, stiffening when she saw that everyone was staring at her. There were so many of them. It looked like everyone who had come to rescue her months ago was there, along with some of the RARE team members. Chase stood next to Angel only a few feet away, both of them watching her in concern. The trembling of her body turned into full blown shaking at the sight of so many people, but she refused to allow the emotions bombarding her to take over.

Her gaze went back to Trigger's, but before she could

reply, she heard someone whisper in shock, "Sharina!"

She swung around to see Trigger's mother standing in the hallway, looking into the room, her gaze wandering over the people inside as she assessed the situation. None of the anxiety, anger, or sorrow that always clung to her before was present. She seemed confident and in control.

Walking forward, Sharina stopped next to them, and Alanna couldn't stop herself from reaching for her.

"I hope you don't mind that I crashed the party, Alpha," Sharina said with a small smile as she took Alanna's hand in hers. "When my son said he was coming here to see you, and Alanna asked to come along, I was worried there might be an issue. I thought I better come just in case my daughter needed me."

"An issue?" Chase frowned in confusion. "We would never hurt Alanna, tigress."

"No, not with you, Chase. With Alanna."

When Sharina glanced over at her, Alanna whispered, "Thank you, Mama. I am having some issues." She was doing better now that both Trigger and Sharina were there with her, but she couldn't help being upset with herself that she couldn't seem to handle a meeting with people in her pack, ones she trusted and knew would never hurt her. Raising her head, she took a deep breath, finding the courage she needed. "I apologize, Angel. I used my gift recently in a way that I never have before, and it is affecting me differently than it normally does. It isn't necessarily that I don't want your touch, it's just that my skin feels like it is crawling, and I just can't accept touch from anyone except my family. I hope you understand."

Angel's face softened with concern. "Of course, sweet bear. I would never force anything on you."

"I know." And she did. Angel had always looked out for her, ever since the first day they met and she went head to head with the council to keep her and Fallon with the White River Wolves pack. The alpha mate would never do anything to harm her.

"How about we all take a seat?" Chase suggested, motioning toward the large conference room table. When everyone was either sitting or leaning against the wall behind the alphas, Chase gave her an encouraging smile. "Can you tell us how you used your gift, Alanna, so we know what to watch for in the future in case you do it again?"

When Alanna hesitated, Sharina leaned forward and placed her forearms on the table. "She healed me, Alpha. I have been a complete emotional wreck since the attack on my streak that took my husband and family from me. I was filled with so much pain and sadness." She paused, "And rage. A ton of rage at the loss of all of my family and friends. I was managing it all at first, but then my son went away to the military, and without him here I had no one and nothing to focus on."

"Damn it," Trigger muttered, and Alanna immediately placed a hand on his thigh in comfort.

"We hadn't been here very long. And even though everyone accepted us and treated us as part of the pack, I got lost in my head. I'd never suffered from anxiety before, but it started then. I was afraid to leave my house, afraid the human faction that killed my streak would come here and slaughter everyone. Afraid, well of everything really. Fear, rage, and sorrow are hard enough emotions to deal with on their own, but all together with deep anxiety thrown in? Life was horrible. I hid in my house and refused to leave. Not even to visit with other pack members. I couldn't handle it."

"I am so sorry, Sharina." Chase reached across the table as if he were going to take her hand but stopped just shy of it. "I failed you."

She shook her head. "No, Alpha, that isn't on you. It was all my fault. I should have asked for help in the very beginning. I knew I needed it, but I was too proud. I won't ever make that mistake again."

While he didn't look convinced, Chase just nodded. "So, Alanna somehow took those emotions away from you like she does other people's pain?"

When Sharina looked over at her Alanna leaned in to Trigger, but forced herself to answer honestly. "When I take someone's pain from them and heal them, their pain becomes mine, but it is even worse. I've never told anyone that, not even Fallon. She knows I feel the pain, but thinks it isn't nearly as bad as what the person I'm healing is feeling. The truth is, I feel it to a much greater extent and I'm down for days, sometimes weeks. It's like I am stuck in darkness and I literally can't move, at all, except to open my eyes. I can't use my psychic abilities. I can't communicate with anyone." She paused and looked over at Trigger with a small smile. "Well, Trigger and I figured out I can answer yes or no questions by blinking once or twice, but that's it." He nodded, his lips curving up slightly.

"We didn't see you for a couple of weeks after you helped Raven. She was really worried about you."

Alanna glanced over to where Jaxson sat at the far end of the long table, his almost always present laptop in front of him. "Yes, that one was hard. Your mate was in so much pain. I hadn't felt anything like that before."

"Saving Nevaeh was worse." She looked over at Phoenix and nodded in agreement. She didn't know what to say. Yes, it was worse, but if she had to do it all over again, she would in a heartbeat. "I am so fucking sorry, Alanna. I never should have asked you to do something like that. I knew there was a danger to you, but I didn't want to lose my baby."

Trigger put his arm around her shoulders and pulled her close, pressing a kiss to the top of her head. "If I've learned anything about my mate in the past few weeks, Phoenix, it's that there was no way you could have stopped her from saving your daughter's life. She is as stubborn as they come, and so damn strong. There is no way she was going to let anything happen to your baby."

"But if I hadn't gone to get her..." Phoenix's voice trailed off, but they all knew exactly what would have happened if he hadn't gotten Alanna.

"If you hadn't gone, Nevaeh wouldn't be here right now," Trigger said, "and that is unacceptable. I was pissed, really pissed, at all of you for thinking it was okay to exchange my mate's life for anyone else's. But the bottom line is, anyone in this room would have given their life for your daughter, me included."

"Hell, yeah we would," Nico stated. "In a heartbeat."

Several voices chimed in agreeing, and Phoenix rasped, "Thanks man. Just, thanks."

"No thanks needed. Just bring Serenity and your little girl over soon. I'm sure my mate would love to see Nevaeh."

A wide grin spread across Phoenix's face. "You got it."

"Now, for the reason we're here," Trigger said, giving

her one last hug before pulling his arm from around her and placing it on the table. "We need your help."

"Anything," Phoenix answered right away. "Anything you need."

"Me too," Jaxson piped up.

"Us too," Sable said, speaking for both herself and her mate. Her eyes gleamed in determination from where she leaned against the wall next to Dax.

"You know Chase and I are in," Angel said, slapping her hand down on the table in front of her. "Tell us what you need."

Alanna frowned, her gaze going to Trigger. She'd never asked him why he was coming to see the alpha. She'd just wanted to be with him. She had no idea what was going on.

"My mate had a vision." Alanna stiffened, her eyes widening as she stared at Trigger. "She said someone is coming for her. Someone who needs help saving a little boy. He's going to take her, and she is going to go with him and help the child because it's what she does. However, this time she doesn't think she will live through it."

"You need us to find this man and eliminate the threat?"

Alanna waited for Trigger to answer Phoenix's question, unsure what she wanted him to say. What would she do if he said yes? She couldn't live with herself if she knew there was a child out there who needed her and she didn't try to help him. But she also didn't want to leave her mate to live his life alone, or leave his mother alone if he chose to follow her into death.

"No. We are going to find him, but not to eliminate

him." He glanced down at her, and then lifted his hand to brush a strand of hair back from her face. "My woman has a gift. One she feels very strongly about using. I fully support her, but I want control of the situation. We find him, see exactly what is wrong with the child, and then we plan. Alanna will do what she can to help the boy, but I will be by her side the entire time. She goes nowhere without me."

"We need all the information we can find," Nico said nodding over to Jaxson. "If anyone can find this guy, it's Jaxson."

Jaxson nodded, opening the laptop in front of him. "I'll need all the information you can recall from your visions, Alanna. Everything you can remember, including every last detail about this guy. Then I will start piecing everything together to narrow it down and find the bastard."

I already know who he is, Alanna whispered into Trigger's mind, for some reason afraid to say it out loud.

Trigger froze, then slowly turned his head to look at her.

What?

I've seen him before, she admitted, glancing nervously around the room and then back to him. *Here in this building.*

Why the hell didn't you say anything to someone?

Her lower lip trembled as she replied, *It wouldn't change anything. It is all still going to happen. I've seen it.*

His eyes never leaving hers, Trigger growled, "I have no psychic abilities and I don't understand how it all works, but can visions change?"

"What?" Rikki asked, cocking her head to the side and raising an eyebrow.

"If Alanna had a vision, can that vision be altered? Or is it going to happen no matter what?"

The entire room was quiet as they all looked at them. It was Nico who replied. "Visions *can* be altered. I always thought mine were set in stone, but I had one when we first came here on the mission to save my daughter, Lily. I was going to be taken by the General."

"I changed it," Rikki interjected, a note of satisfaction in her voice, ignoring the low growl of her mate, Jeremiah, from where he sat next to her. "I knew there was no way Nico would survive if the General's men got to him. He was already mated to Jenna, and the General's plan was to throw him into a breeding program. There was no way it could have happened. So, I used my ability to read objects and was able to pull a vision from it showing Nico's vision. And instead of them capturing Nico, I manipulated the situation and took his place."

Alanna's pulse was racing as she listened to them talk. She couldn't believe what she was hearing. There could be a way to alter her vision. A way for her to help the boy and still live a long life with her mate. She had no idea how, but maybe, just maybe there was hope.

Trigger...

What is his name, Alanna?

She hesitated only a moment before she said out loud, "Dominic Reeves."

"Son of a bitch," Angel snapped, slamming her fist on the table. "I told that asshole to reach out if he needs help, and instead he is planning on kidnapping one of our own? I will kill him myself!"

"I need the background, Angel," Trigger said, his eyes on Alanna's. She loved how he didn't look away from her.

It was as if he knew she needed that connection to him right now, if only for a moment.

"He came here supposedly on council orders to check on Alanna and Fallon when they arrived. I knew it was a lie. Dominic is not a council enforcer. His dad is Dante Reeves, one of the council members, but there was no way in hell he would support Dominic in something like this. I looked into his mind when he was here and I could tell a member of his family was sick, but I don't have the details. I'm sorry, I was focused on finding Chase at that time. I should have dug deeper."

"I got it," Jackson said, his fingers still flying over the keyboard in front of him. "It's his grandson, Parker Reeves. The boy has cancer. It's bad. Spread throughout his entire body."

"Cancer?" Sharina asked in confusion. "Shifters can't get cancer."

"Parker is human. He's eight years old. His mother and Dominic's son got together right after Parker was born. His biological father wanted nothing to do with him, but he was killed in a car accident a year later, so that isn't pertinent information."

"Where is he?" Trigger asked, covering Alanna's hand with his, finally tearing his gaze from hers to look over at Jaxson.

"Just a couple of hours from here, in a small town I've never heard of. Carion."

"How much longer does the child have?" Alanna asked, her heart breaking for little Parker and his family.

Jaxson raised his head, a grave look in his eyes. "Not long, Alanna. The doctors are saying two to three weeks at the most."

"It sounds to me like you better get a plan of action quick, and then we need to get moving," Sharina said calmly, covering Alanna's other hand with hers. "Alanna and I will be going home now so she can rest. She needs to be in top form when she attempts to heal this child. We will leave the mission planning to you and my son."

"Are you planning on going with us, Sharina?"

Sharina stood and Alanna reluctantly rose beside her. "Of course, Alpha. If you think I will allow my son's mate to do something like this without me by her side, then you are dead wrong. I go where she goes."

I want to be with you, Alanna protested when Sharina turned to leave. She was exhausted, and knew it was best to go back home, but she wanted Trigger with her.

I'm needed here, sweet mate, but I will be home as soon as I can. Sleep in my bed this time.

Your bed?

It's where you belong.

Can I...

Can you what, sweetheart?

Alanna glanced quickly over to the others who seemed to be waiting patiently. Her heart jumped when she realized they knew exactly what was going on, because a lot of them were telepathic, like her. They knew she was talking to her mate, and they weren't rushing her.

She flushed, ducking her head, and then she asked softly, *Would it be okay if I stopped by my apartment and brought some things to your house?*

You can pack up the entire thing and move it, mate. I don't plan on letting you ever sleep there again.

Alanna burst into laughter, shaking her head at him

before turning to follow Sharina from the room. "I'll see you at home, mate."

Trigger chuckled, "Get some rest, sweetheart."

Looking back, she gave him one last radiant smile and a small wave before leaving the room.

10

It was close to midnight before Trigger finally let himself into his house. It took a lot longer than he thought it would to come up with any sort of plan, but at least they had one he felt halfway comfortable with. No matter how he went about it, after going over all the doctor reports Jaxson somehow managed to dig up, he had to admit the outcome for his mate did not seem incredibly positive. The disease was extensive, taking over Parker's entire body. Deadly and destructive. If Alanna took all of that into her, or whatever the fuck it was that she did, how could she overcome it?

It didn't matter. Trigger would be there for her, support her, and fight like the devil himself for her, but there was no way in hell he was going to lose her. Her death was not an option.

"How did it go, son?"

Trigger sighed, grabbing a bottle of water from the fridge and walking over to sit across from his mother at the kitchen table. He should have known she'd wait up for him. She was his rock; always had been. He didn't care if she decided she didn't want to step foot outside the house ever again after all of this was over. He would continue to love her and look after her, the way she had him for so many years.

"It went," he said with another deep sigh. "Any way you look at it, the kid is dying. His body is riddled with cancer. If I understand what Alanna does correctly, to save him, she is going to have to take all of that from him, along with all his pain." He winced and raked a hand through his hair in frustration. "I wish we had more time so I could make sure she was fully recovered from saving Nevaeh's life, but Parker needs her now."

"She saved that little baby, and then was still recovering when she helped me," his mother whispered, lowering her gaze to the table, her brow creased in a frown. There was so much guilt and shame in her voice and her fingers were clutched tightly into small fists.

"From what I can tell, it's a totally different thing." Tilting his head back, Trigger took a long drink of his water before setting the bottle back on the table. He'd been neglecting his own needs since bringing Alanna home, and knew he was slightly dehydrated and needed to eat. He was starving and couldn't remember the last time he'd sat down and had a full meal. "What she did for you isn't hurting her, Mama. Not physically. She was up, walking around, talking. She couldn't do any of that after helping Nevaeh or Raven."

"She ate some dinner tonight too," Sharina shared softly. "We stopped at her place on the way home and she packed all of her things in a bag to bring here. She didn't have much. Her bedroom was empty, for the most part. A few outfits, a pair of slippers, some toiletry items, and a couple of books. No pictures, no personal things."

"She didn't want to accumulate a bunch of stuff when she didn't think she was going to live." Trigger hated that thought, but knew he was right. Why collect things when you weren't going to be around to enjoy them?

"Well, dammit, she's going to live a long, happy life here with us. We will buy her all the special things she wants." His mother's eyes were bright and wet with unshed tears. "She's ours now to love and spoil."

"Did you know Alanna was the one who's been giving you the little gifts when I'm gone?" Trigger asked, thinking about how sweet his adorable mate was. So tiny, with a heart bigger than anyone he knew, even though she'd never grown up with any kind of love or caring herself.

"No." His mother laughed softly, shaking her head, a tender look in her eyes. "That woman's generosity knows no bounds. She has nothing to her name herself, but she reaches out to a woman who is too terrified to leave her house and gives her special things."

"So damn sweet with a heart of gold."

"So, what are you waiting for?" Sharina asked with a raise of an eyebrow. "Go, claim your mate, son." When he hesitated, unsure if it was the right time to do something like that with all that Alanna was going through, his mother growled, "You need to cement that mate bond, Trigger. You need a way to pull her out of what she calls the darkness so it doesn't consume her after she heals that child. Only you will be able to reach her, but you will need that bond to do it."

Trigger stiffened, the hand that was just reaching for

his bottle of water freezing midway to it. "What do you mean?"

"You know your father and I weren't true mates, so I've never experienced it for myself, but my parents were. One of the times they were trying to talk me out of marrying William, they told me that when you find your mate and complete the bond it's as if your souls merge together and are complete. There is an invisible tether between the two mates, and the only way it would ever be broken is if one of them dies. They said you can feel each other through that bond. Which only stands to reason, if something were to go terribly wrong, and Alanna were to be leaving this world, there might be a way you could somehow hold on tight to her and bring her back."

"Holy shit. I didn't know. I mean, there's a connection between us now like I've never felt before, but I didn't know it would become even stronger once we..." He trailed off as he thought about what his mom had said. Could she be right? Would their bond be strong enough to save Alanna if everything went to hell like he thought it was going to?

No one in the meeting had said a word about the bond, and they would have known he and Alanna hadn't fully completed it yet. The lack of mate marks would have given it away, not to mention the fact that their scents hadn't changed. When a couple mated, their scents merged, becoming unique to the two of them.

Before Trigger could continue that thought, there was a light knock on his door. He inhaled deeply and frowned when he caught the scent of his alpha, the alpha mate, and one other person he couldn't quite place. He knew he'd smelled the male's scent before, but he couldn't recall when or where.

Rising, he strode quickly to the door and opened it, stepping outside when he saw Jinx standing out back with Chase and Angel. Not that he didn't want the other man in his house, but he'd heard someone say once that the wolf didn't care for enclosed places, especially ones he'd never been in before.

"Trigger, sorry to drop by so late. My son wanted to talk to you and said it needed to be tonight."

"No problem, Alpha." Trigger nodded over to the man who was staring at him, no expression on his face. "Jinx, it's good to see you."

Jinx's deep brown eyes flashed an emerald green before he gave a short nod in return. "You need to claim your bear and cement the mate bond. It will tie her to you and help us get her out of the darkness after she completes her task of saving the child."

"My mom was just saying the same thing." Trigger knew the man was smart, wicked smart, and valued his opinion. There was no doubt in his mind that if Jinx said to do it, then it needed to be done. Suddenly, he froze as he fully realized what the wolf had just said. "Us? You mean you're going to come with us? Help my mate?"

Jinx shrugged, his gaze still blank. The man had lived a life of hell, worse than anything Trigger had been through. Trigger knew he wasn't trying to be a prick, he was just heavily guarding himself, which was understandable. "It's what pack does."

A slow smile slid across Trigger's lips, and he reached out a hand to the young man. He waited patiently while Jinx looked at it in confusion before slowly sliding his own hand into it. Tugging him forward, Trigger gave him a quick side hug, along with a slap on the back, and then stepped back. "Yes, it is what pack does. Thank you, Jinx. Having your help right now means everything to me."

The man was a fucking assassin for first the General, and now Ebony, both who were evil to the core. But to RARE and the White River Wolves pack, he was so much more. Friend, brother, family. He'd saved many of them when their lives were in danger. Fought for them, no matter the cost to himself. The fact that he was standing on Trigger's back porch right now, offering his help with what was to come, just raised Alanna's survival rate extensively. He had no idea how to thank the wolf.

"I won't forget this. Ever. You need anything, anything at all, you call on me. I've got your back."

"I make no promises, tiger."

"I didn't ask for any. Just you stepping up to offer your help is enough."

Jinx's hard gaze could have been made from granite, but Trigger knew he was deliberately hiding any emotion he felt. He would have to, given the life he lived. Trigger was in awe of the shifter, had been since the first time he saw him and heard stories of the man in action.

"I think it's time you let us leave, and you get your business taken care of, son."

Trigger glanced over to see his mother standing beside him, a small bag in her hand. "What are you doing?"

"You need time alone with your mate. I need to get some sleep tonight, which I know won't happen if I stay here."

"Mom." He didn't like the thought of her staying anywhere else. She hadn't left the house in as long as he could remember. How was she going to leave and stay in a place that wasn't her home?

Sharina laughed, shaking her head. "I'm just going to Fallon's. It's only for one night. I talked to her about it earlier and she invited me to sleep in Alanna's old room."

"How are you going to handle that?"

Sharina's face softened and she raised her hand to rest against the side of his face. "Your mate healed me this morning, Trigger. I don't know what she did, hell I don't think she even knows, but I'm not afraid to leave the house. I'm not terrified of staying with someone else at their place. I'm not angry with the whole world or depressed enough to take my own life." When he bit out a curse in alarm, she whispered, "I'm not like that anymore, son. I'm okay now. Alanna is a gift. She saved me, and now it's our turn to save her. Go, it's time you claim your mate."

When he still hesitated, Jinx stepped forward. "She's right. Your bear is a gift from the Gods to you. You need to take tonight to bind your souls so you can be together for many years to come. I'll make sure your mother gets to Fallon's safely. I will even watch over her tonight in case she gets scared or nervous and needs to come back home. If she does, I will bring her, but she won't. She will be fine." Jinx raised a fist to his chest, covering his heart with it. "I give you my word."

Fuck, the guy was hard core. Trigger knew if he gave his word on something, it was a done deal. That was it. It hadn't escaped his notice that Jinx didn't give his word to save Alanna, but he appreciated the fact that the man wasn't going to promise something he might not be able to follow through on. It made Trigger trust him even more.

"You'll bring her back in the morning?"

"We'll be here at ten."

Ten. He could work with that.

"Come hungry. Breakfast will be ready."

He was surprised to see the small grin Jinx gave him before the man motioned to Sharina and they turned to leave. They moved through the darkness side by side, but Jinx still looked like a lone wolf.

"When is he going to officially become part of the pack?"

Angel sighed, a sad look crossing her features as she leaned into Chase. "Your guess is as good as ours."

"He'll come when he's ready," Chase said, leaning down to place a kiss on his mate's forehead. "He's a man with a lot on his mind right now. Too many responsibilities for one person to handle."

"But always stepping up to help others." Trigger shook his head as he watched his mother and Jinx until he couldn't see them anymore. "No matter how this turns out, I hope he knows how grateful I am that he's willing to join us, considering his own private hell he's living through."

"He knows."

11

Alanna felt the light brush of fingers as they started at her ankle and ghosted up her leg and over her hip, stopping at the waistband of her sleep shorts. She inhaled deeply, loving how her mate's scent surrounded her.

She'd known the moment he'd entered the room. Heard him slip out of his clothes, then move to the bed. Felt it when he slid the covers down and off her. Her pulse fluttered wildly as his fingers stoked over the skin on her sides and up, taking her shirt with them.

"So beautiful, smooth, soft. Mine." The words were spoken softly, in a deep, rough tone of possession.

"Yours," she agreed with a whisper, as she raised her arms so he could remove the pajama top, sliding it over her head and off.

He stared at her for a moment, his dark hooded gaze moving from her eyes to her lips and down lower over the flushed skin on her neck, then down even more until he stopped on her chest. Her firm, round breasts all but begging for his touch as she panted his name in desire. She wanted him, *needed him,* to do *something.*

Alanna cried out, her back arching off the bed when Trigger suddenly bent his head, his mouth closing over one of her nipples, sending a shockwave through her body. She'd never felt anything like it. Her hands went to his thick dark hair, and she slid her fingers into the soft strands, clutching them tightly. He pulled back slightly, nipping at the nipple before stroking it with his tongue. Her cries grew louder as his tongue stroked over her nipple, and then he tugged on it gently before sucking it into his mouth. So hot and wet, sending another wave of desire coursing through her.

"Trigger," she gasped, holding his head to her chest as she pushed her breast up into him. "Please. Please!" She had no idea what she was begging for. All she knew was she needed more. More of whatever he was doing to her to make her core clench tightly in pleasure.

"I've got you, baby."

She made a sound of protest when his mouth left her breast, but it turned into a low moan when he captured the nipple of her other breast in his mouth and gave it the same attention he'd given the first one. Alanna knew she was being loud, her moans and cries filling the air, but she couldn't help it. She couldn't hold back, especially when he bit down lightly, causing her to throw her head back as she bit back a scream.

"I want to hear you, mate," Trigger growled, his hands going to the waistband of her shorts. "All of those little moans, those gasps, those screams, they're all mine. I want to hear them. Give me what's mine."

"Oh God!" Alanna cried out as Trigger trailed his lips

down her stomach. His words alone nearly brought her to the edge. She loved how possessive he sounded. How growly and demanding he was. She wanted more.

Trigger's teeth nipped, his tongue licked, and his fingers stroked as he pushed her pajamas down her legs. When his hands spread her thighs open and his tongue stroked through her lower lips, she couldn't hold in the scream that erupted from her throat.

"Fuck yeah," he snarled as he found her clit, licking and sucking at the small nub. "Mine! All mine!"

Her hands clenched tightly in his hair, holding him to her while he continued to play her clit with his mouth as he slid one finger into her wet channel. Alanna bucked her hips, begging for more. Needing more from him.

Something was building inside her, something she'd only read about in sensual romance novels but never actually felt herself. Trigger slipped another finger inside, moving them in and out as he stroked her clit back and forth with his tongue. When he added a third finger, there was a slight pain, but it quickly turned to pleasure.

Suddenly, it all became too much and she flew apart, screaming his name as she came hard. Her entire body was shaking, pulsing with desire, and she wanted more.

Trigger slid his fingers from her and looked up to meet her eyes. His were dark and full of heat. And when he raised his fingers to his mouth, the ones that had just been inside her, and licked them clean, she couldn't help the deep moan that slipped out.

Slowly, he crawled up her body, lowering his forehead to rest it in the crook of her neck. A shudder ran through his body as he placed the head of his thick, hard cock at her entrance. Slowly, he began to push forward, working his way inside her. Alanna slid her hands over his back and up to his shoulder, her nails digging in when she began to feel slight pain. He was big, stretching her, filling her.

Trigger stopped moving for a moment, raising his head and finding her mouth with his. He rasped her name quietly, almost reverently, before stroking his tongue over her lips and then pushing his way inside her mouth to find hers. He ate at her mouth as he began to move again, sliding deeper inside her, not stopping until he came to the barrier that showed him she'd saved herself for her mate. For him.

Breathing heavily, Trigger pulled back and placed his forehead on hers, reaching back to grab one of her hands and lacing their fingers together. "You are giving me a gift, my mate. One I will cherish for all our lives."

A tremulous smile crossed her lips, her eyes misting with tears. She hoped they had a long life together. She wanted to know what it felt like to be cherished.

Leaning back, Trigger kissed her gently. Then locking eyes with her, he pushed through the barrier, not stopping until he bottomed out. Alanna bit into her lip to stifle her moan of pain. She'd known it would hurt the first time, but it wasn't as bad as she feared. Soon, the pain was ebbing away and pleasure began building.

Trigger stayed still, his eyes on hers until she slowly began to move her hips, rocking up into him. Lowering his head, he feathered a soft kiss over her lips, nipping at them gently, then sucking the fuller bottom one into his mouth. Alanna's heartbeat accelerated and gasped his name as she bucked her hips again, trying to make him move.

Slowly breaking the kiss, Trigger squeezed the hand he was still holding as he rasped, "Okay?"

Alanna nodded, moving restlessly beneath him.

"I need the words, baby. I need to know you aren't hurting."

Alanna licked her lips, her head going back, bearing her neck to him as she pushed up into him again. "Please. Trigger. I need you!"

"Fuck," he growled, burying his head into the side of her neck as he finally began to move. Slow, deep thrusts at first that became steadily faster and faster.

She loved the way he felt inside her. So hard, thick, big. Heat rolled over her skin, her body trembling as that feeling of passion began to build in her again. The one that made her soar last time. She wanted that again.

She reached for it, chased it, her hips moving faster, meeting him thrust for thrust. Her fangs dropped, and a low growl began to rumble in her chest, an answering one coming from him.

Alanna's eyes lowered to where his neck and shoulder met. The place where she wanted to leave her mark. The thought of it had small growls leaving her throat, and Trigger groaned loudly when she raked her nails down his back. He grunted when she dug her nails into his skin, his hands finding her hips and holding them tightly as he took over, pistoning in and out of her tight heat. Suddenly, she was flying apart again, his name on her lips. Her mouth found his skin, her teeth sinking deep as she claimed what was hers.

Trigger threw his head back and roared as he came inside her, and then he found her shoulder and bit, leaving his mate mark for all to see. The second his fangs penetrated her skin, Alanna came again, squeezing his cock hard as she growled, her own teeth still embedded in his shoulder.

It was a long moment before either of them moved, neither one wanting to separate from the other. Finally, Trigger removed his fangs. "Alanna," he rasped, as he lapped gently at the mark he'd left, removing the small amount of blood left behind. "My beautiful mate. My world. My everything."

Alanna wrapped her arms tightly around Trigger's neck, holding him to her as she stroked her tongue over her own mark on him. She gasped, the air hissing out of her lungs when she felt the moment their souls seemed to merge, then click into place. Suddenly, she could feel him in ways she hadn't before. It was as if they were tied together, something connecting them, something that could never be broken.

They were completely bonded, for better or worse. Their fate was tied together. If one left this world, the other would follow. There was no turning back, but Alanna found she didn't want to. She wanted to move forward. She wanted a life with her mate. Children. A large family. And she was going to fight for it, no matter what she had to do.

12

Trigger watched as the first subtle rays of sunlight slipped through his window. He'd always liked to watch the sunrise. To see the beginning of a new day. He lived his life under the mindset that even though you couldn't change the past, if you focused on the present, you could produce a better future. It had taken him several long years to get to that point after what happened to his streak, but he'd finally made it. He now chose to live his life helping others to the best of his ability, in whatever way he was needed. He didn't waste time on the things he couldn't change, and concentrated on the things he could.

He was a gruff person and didn't tell many people about his private life, past or present. His alpha knew what he'd been through, the things he had done, which meant Angel did too because mates didn't keep secrets from each other. And if they did, they shouldn't. He firmly believed that, which meant he had a few things to talk to Alanna about this morning. Important things that they should have discussed before exchanging mate bites, but he'd lost his damn mind when he first ran his hands over her soft, silky skin and forgot about everything except touching her. Loving her. Claiming her.

Trigger knew she cared about him, he saw it in her eyes, felt it in her touch, but the things he needed to tell her could change the way she looked at him. It scared him, but he refused to hold any of himself back from her. She deserved him to be all in, and he hoped she felt the same. As far as he knew, she hadn't kept anything from him, but if she had, maybe his opening up would help her as well.

Or maybe it would make her run for the hills.

Sighing deeply, Trigger glanced down to where his sweet bear lay against his chest, surprised to see her awake and looking up at him with a soft, tender look in her beautiful brown eyes. A small smile appeared, and she raised her hand to stroke it over the dark scruff on his jaw.

"You're thinking awfully hard, mate. Do you want to talk about it?"

He returned her smile with a forced one of his own and leaned down to place a kiss on her forehead. She rested her chin on her arm, her warm gaze never leaving his as she raised one eyebrow and waited patiently.

"My mom told you about my streak," he started slowly, his eyes going to the window, unable to look at her as he made his confession. "We lost everyone that day. It was horrible. I still have nightmares sometimes. All the blood. My grandparents gunned down, each with a bullet between their eyes. My father, his body being sliced into as I lifted my mom over my shoulder and ran like he told me to. I glanced back once, wanting to defy his order no matter how much it would piss him off, and there were three guys on him then. Tearing into him. Mutilating him."

Alanna gasped, and she slid a hand up his chest and around his neck, holding him to her. She stayed silent, as if she knew he needed to get out what he wanted to say and might stop if she interrupted him.

A shudder ran though his body as Trigger closed his eyes and remembered that fateful day. The one that took everything and everyone from him, except his beloved mama. "It was too late for my father, but not for Mama. I ran and ran, ignoring her sobs of pain and her begging to take her back and let her die with my father. I did what he wanted instead and got her the hell out of there." He paused, his arm around her waist pulling her tighter to him. "I didn't stop moving, first on foot and then stealing different vehicles, swapping them out for new ones every few hundred miles. I kept going until we were in Colorado."

Alanna placed a soft kiss on his chest, right over his heart, but still stayed quiet.

"We were hiding out in Denver. I was doing some things I wasn't proud of, illegal things, to make money. Mostly underground fighting, but I also stole food, clothes, blankets, things we needed to survive. Until the day Chase caught me." Trigger chuckled as he remembered that dark night that seemed so long ago. "I'd lost a fight the night before and didn't have any money, but we needed food. I was weak because it'd been a couple of days since we'd really eaten anything. I was in the process of grabbing a loaf of bread from a street vender when a hand snaked out and grabbed my wrist, holding it in a grip too tight for me to break away from."

That day, meeting Chase and a couple of his enforcers, had been the turning point in his life. He would never be able to pay the alpha back for what he did for both him and his mother. For taking a chance on him after his entire world had imploded.

"Chase saved us that day. He brought us home with him. Made us a part of his pack. Turned my life around, removing me from the destructive path I was on." Trigger ran his hand down Alanna's long, soft hair, loving how it went all the way to her waist, stopping just above her luscious bottom. He wanted to grab those round globes and pull her up to him, sink inside her warm heat and forget about what he was telling her, but he knew he couldn't. She needed to know everything.

"We were here for just over a year before I decided to go into the military. I wish I could say it was for honorable reasons, like I wanted to serve my country, but it wasn't." He hesitated before admitting, "I had a plan, Alanna. I enlisted because I wanted training only the military could provide." And no part of him regretted it.

"You wanted to find the people who murdered your father, family, and streak."

Trigger lowered his gaze to meet hers, thinking he would see condemnation there, but all he saw was love and understanding. He nodded, lifting a hand to cup her cheek. "I did two tours, the last three years were as an assassin for the government. I was a killer, taking out whoever they told me to. I didn't ask why, I didn't question any of my orders, I just followed through on them as I was trained to do."

He'd hated it. He had no problem taking a life if he was protecting someone, but the life of an assassin, even if it was sanctioned by the United States government, was not one he ever wanted to repeat. It had served its purpose though, helping him reach his ultimate goal.

"You did your job, Trigger," Alanna whispered, turning her head to place a kiss in the palm of his hand.

"A job I went into with one sole purpose in mind," Trigger growled, closing his eyes tightly for a moment as all the memories from so long ago came rushing back. "I jumped in feet first with my eyes wide open. I wanted them to train me to be the ultimate killer. I wanted to learn all the skills I could so I could go hunting when I got out."

He needed her to see what he'd done. To understand who and what he was. What he could be if those he loved were threatened. What would happen if anyone hurt her or tried to take her from him.

He opened his eyes, looking straight into hers as he confessed, "And I did, Alanna. I hunted down every last one of those bastards I could find. It was hard at first. I didn't have a lot to go on. But I remembered their faces, their scents. All of the names I heard that day. I got online and searched every single thing I could find regarding human radical groups, weeding out the ones that were going after shifters. It took me months to find the faction I was looking for, but I finally did. And then I stalked them, taking them out one by one until the very last son of a bitch ate one of my bullets. I got rid of the bodies in a way that they will never be found. When it was finally over, I came here to my mother and the White River Wolves."

Her expression never changed, not once as he told her his most guarded secret. Not even his mother knew what he'd done, how many lives he'd taken.

"Does the alpha know?" Alanna asked him softly.

"I suspect he might, but I've never brought it up, and he's never asked." When he'd finally come home, Chase had welcomed him back, even throwing a party celebrating his return. Trigger caught the alpha watching him closely over the first year, but no one brought up where he'd been within the timeframe of when he got out of the military, to when he'd finally shown up at the compound.

Chase had offered Trigger an enforcer job, and after he'd proven himself, he was asked to be a part of his elite team. The alpha trusted him, and Trigger vowed to never betray the man's trust. If Chase ever asked, he would tell him the full truth of what he'd done, but he doubted the conversation would ever come up.

"Thank you, mate, for confiding in me," Alanna said, her eyes glittering with emotion. "For trusting me with a part of yourself that you've never let anyone else see."

Trigger frowned, his eyes narrowing on her. Did she not hear what he'd just told her? Didn't she realize what it meant? She was innocent in so many ways, and as much as he wanted to accept her easy reply, he couldn't just let it go. He needed her eyes wide open, seeing exactly what he'd done.

"Alanna, I need you to understand what I did. Who I am. What I am capable of."

"I do understand." Alanna pushed herself up on her hands and knees and moved up his body until her face hovered over his, her neatly trimmed mound sliding over his hard cock. He groaned, his hips raising up, his shaft rubbing against her. He couldn't help it. No matter how serious their discussion was, his body wanted hers. He wanted inside her so fucking bad. "I see *you*, Trigger Michelson."

"I hunted them down, Alanna," he ground out through gritted teeth. "I killed them, straight up murdered them out of revenge."

Her face softened, and it felt as if her love was reaching out to him, surrounding him, pushing its way inside him. Love. Something he hadn't felt from anyone except his mother in so long. Trigger began to shake uncontrollably as he absorbed the feeling, needing it more than he'd ever needed anything in his life. Knowing he would never be able to survive without it again.

"I don't care why you did what you did, Trigger. I look at it differently than you seem to. Do you realize how many lives you saved by removing those vile, evil people from this earth? How many men, women, and children are here today because of you? No matter your reason for doing it, there are so many people still here on earth today because of your actions. People like those monsters never change. They would never have stopped their killing."

"But..."

"No!" Alanna growled, her brown eyes spitting fire. "You. Saved. Lives. Hundreds, if not thousands, of lives. You are a damn hero, mate, and I refuse to let you think differently." She clutched tightly to his shoulders, her nails digging into his skin. "I honestly can't remember the last time I felt safe, Trigger. My parents never protected me from my brother. He threatened me daily, hurt me both emotionally and physically, but they didn't care. No one has ever stood up for me, put me first, except for Fallon when she contacted the council on my behalf. No one has ever made me feel the way you make me feel. Like I matter. Like the world could go up in flames around me, but you would protect me from it all. Keep me safe. Eliminate anything or anyone who threatens me." Leaning down, she rubbed her cheek against his, then stilled as she whispered into his ear, "I love you, Trigger, so damn much. I want to be with you, stand by you in this life and the next. Be yours forever. An eternity."

"Fuck. Alanna."

It was all he got out before she was moving. Grasping his cock in her hand and then sliding down on the hard, straining length, taking him deep inside her and coating him with her slick heat. He let out a low, deep growl that had been building in his chest as she began to move, squeezing his cock so tightly he knew he wouldn't last long.

Trigger bunched her hair in his fist and held her head still as he captured her mouth with his. Licking, biting, sucking her sexy, pouty pink lips as she rode his cock. Claiming her as she claimed him. He held her hip in a firm grip but let her have control. As much as he wanted to take over, he wanted to give her this more.

She'd accepted him. All of him. More than that, she'd handed over her heart to him to keep safe. She had no idea what that meant to him.

Slipping past her lips, Trigger mapped the inside of her mouth with his tongue. Stroking, sucking on her tongue, loving her taste.

Tearing her mouth from his, Alanna placed her palms on his chest and pushed herself up, throwing her head back as little cries poured from her driving him insane.

He loved how loud she was, how passionate. She didn't hold anything back from him, and it made him harder, drove him higher.

His hands went to her round, firm breasts, cradling them in his palms. He rubbed his thumbs on her pretty pink nipples, loving the way her body trembled and she called out his name. He groaned when his cock was bathed in wetness and had to fight for control.

Alanna looked down at him, her eyes glowing with her animal, her mouth open showing her sexy as fuck fangs. She was so breathtaking, so beautiful, and he wanted those pearly white teeth embedded deep in his skin. He felt his own fangs drop, and bucked his hips up before he could stop himself. His hands fell to her hips, holding her still as he lost the battle and began thrusting into her warm, wet sheath hard and fast.

Alanna's gaze, hot with lust, went to where she'd left her mark on him the night before, and she bared her fangs, growling loudly. Her nails raked over his chest, then dug in deep, her eyes darkening until they were almost black.

"Fuck, mate," Trigger snarled as she suddenly stiffened, and then she was contracting around him, fisting his cock so tightly he couldn't have stopped his own orgasm if he wanted to. "Bite me." No sooner had the words left his mouth than he felt her lips on his shoulder, her teeth breaking the skin. He came so hard, the only thing he could do was sink his own fangs deep into her shoulder and hold on tight.

It was a long moment before he could catch his breath, and even longer before he finally slid his teeth from her flesh. He held her close, encircled in his arms, not wanting to move. Soon enough they would have to face the day, but not yet. Right now was for them.

I love you, Trigger.

He loved hearing those words in his head, so soft and intimate. He would never tire of it.

I love you too, sweet mate. For all eternity.

She'd said she wanted to be his for an eternity, and he was going to do everything in his power to make that happen.

13

Alanna stared across the kitchen at the man who looked like he would rather be anywhere else than inside their home. He stood close to the door, his deep brown eyes flashing to a stunning green hue and then back. She could see the hilt of a sword at his back, a gun on one hip, and several pockets down the side of his black pants that she was sure held other various weapons.

"Thank you for staying and watching over me last night, Jinx. I really appreciate it. I slept like a baby knowing you were there."

"You're welcome, Ma'am." The word ma'am seemed awkward coming from him, but it was obvious he was trying to be polite.

She'd never actually met him, but Alanna knew who he was. She'd heard rumors about him floating around the compound since she'd moved in. Jinx, first the General's assassin, and now Ebony's. Angel and Steele Maddox's son. A man with abilities that surpassed anyone she'd ever heard before.

Alanna had also seen him one time before — the night Chase and Angel had their mating ceremony. Chase had introduced him as Angel's son, which made him Chase's now as well. The son of an alpha, one who didn't think he was worthy of the title, but Alanna knew the truth. Jinx was more than worthy.

"Won't you come in and have breakfast with us?" Sharina asked, motioning to the table as she gave him a warm smile.

When his gaze swept the room, stopping on her for just a quick moment, Alanna's empath abilities suddenly emerged, like they did sometimes around intense emotion. She felt his hesitation, his nervousness. A bit of that anxiety she'd suffered through herself when she'd taken it from Sharina. She also felt his resolve to do what he felt was right. His determination to endure whatever he had to for them. For pack. No matter how much he didn't want to be inside their house for any length of time.

"Actually," Alanna said, crossing the room to open the door and step out onto the back porch, "I would love to eat out here this morning. It's so beautiful, and I've never eaten breakfast outside." It was all true, he would scent no lie. She loved being outdoors, and even though it was chilly, they were shifters and would be fine. They wouldn't even really notice it.

"Oh, what a great idea!" Sharina said excitedly. "It's been so long since I've enjoyed a meal outside. William and I used to go on picnics all of the time when we were dating." A fond smile appeared, her hand going to rest on her cheek as her eyes glowed with happiness at the fond memory. "There was this quiet, peaceful place down by the lake near where we lived that we went to. It's where he proposed to me."

"I remember that place," Trigger said as he removed more pancakes from the griddle, placing them on a large plate.

Alanna slipped past Jinx again, reaching out to place a hand on his arm and squeezing it gently on her way by. "Why don't you wait outside for us, Jinx? I'm going to grab some things quick to set the table and will be right there."

Jinx's eyes narrowed in suspicion, but all he did was nod and step through the back door, his need to be outside overriding everything else.

"Shit, I forgot about that," Trigger muttered, sliding the last of the pancakes onto the plate.

"What?" Sharina asked in confusion as she lifted another plate already filled with eggs.

"He doesn't like to be indoors." Trigger grabbed a plate of bacon, and the one with pancakes.

Sharina's eyes widened, her hand going to her mouth. "I didn't know. He stayed out on the patio last night, but I didn't think anything of it."

"He's fine," Alanna told them, her arms full of paper plates, plastic silverware, and napkins she'd found in the pantry. She wanted to direct their attention somewhere else. Jinx didn't need them talking about him when he wasn't in the room. He deserved better. "That man is as tough as they come. He isn't one to let fear control his life. Now, let's eat."

She breezed out the door and over to the patio table, ignoring the way she knew Jinx's calculating gaze was following her. She refused to make him feel uncomfortable just because he didn't like enclosed places.

Hell, she felt a bit claustrophobic at times herself. Especially after what her brother did to her when she was thirteen. The bastard had threatened to bury her alive if she didn't follow his orders after she'd told him no. Even going so far as to shove her in a box and nail it shut with just a few holes that allowed her to breathe. She'd stayed in the box for a full night, filled with terror at the thought that Doug would actually follow through with his threat that time. It had been horrible, but somehow she knew it wasn't anything compared to what Jinx had endured over the years.

Alanna took a seat next to her mate as she struggled to lock that memory down tight. One day she would tell Trigger about her past, her life with her psychotic brother, but not now. It wasn't that she didn't want him to know, they just had bigger things to worry about, like a child to save.

Her fingers shook as she reached for a pancake, and Trigger's brow creased in concern as he watched her. She smiled brightly, her eyes going to her plate. "Tell me what the plan is."

"Plan?"

She glanced up at Trigger, and then over to Jinx. "With Parker."

"You haven't told her?" Jinx asked, his hands resting on his thighs. He hadn't reached for any of the food. Hadn't touched the table at all.

Trigger shook his head. "She was asleep when I got home. We've been busy since she woke up."

Jinx nodded, glancing down at the food.

Shit. I can't eat this.

Alanna froze as the wolf's thoughts came to her.

I knew I should have just left. Now I'm going to offend someone. Fuck.

Images slid into her mind of a young boy sitting in a corner, his arms wrapped tightly around his legs. He couldn't have been more than four. He was being punished for forgetting a lesson. Something to do with poison. He was in so much pain. His stomach cramping over and over again. Sweat covered his body. His skin felt as if he were on fire. He was afraid but had to hide his fear or the outcome would be even worse.

Fuck, just do it. They invited you. You want to be here. Eat, dammit. It's not like they would ever try and hurt you.

When Jinx slowly reached for his fork, Alanna rested her hand on his and guided it down to the table. His closed into a tight fist, hers laying just on top of it. When Trigger and Sharina's eyes went to where she held him, Alanna shook her head once.

"Tell me the plan, mate."

Let it go, she whispered into Trigger's mind. *Please.*

Something in her voice must have gotten through to him because Trigger gave a slight nod, then took a drink of his milk before replying. "Instead of waiting around for Dominic to show up, we've decided the best course of action is to go to him. Unfortunately, the consensus is Parker doesn't have much longer, so we think it's best if we go today."

"Today?" Alanna whispered in shock, slowly removing her hand from Jinx's. When she let go, he pulled his away from the table, once again placing it on his thigh. She was suddenly lost as to what to do. How to feel. She'd thought she would have more time.

"Yes. Parker needs us now, Alanna. Doc Josie looked over all of his scans and said, in her professional opinion, his doctors are wrong. The boy isn't going to last through the weekend."

The weekend. Today was Friday. Trigger was right, they had to go now.

Picking up Jinx's plate as nonchalantly as she could, Alanna slid it under her own, then moved his silverware over by hers. Out of sight, out of mind.

"When do we leave?"

"After we eat," Trigger said quietly. "Unless you would prefer to go later this afternoon. He is only a couple of hours from here, but I wanted time to talk to Dominic and Parker's parents before you work your magic. And I figured you would want to talk to Parker."

"Yes," Alanna agreed as she made herself begin to eat again. The food tasted like cardboard now, but she would need to keep her strength up for what was to come. And who knew when she would get another meal.

She forced back tears that wanted to fall as she gripped her fork tightly. Even though she knew she needed to do whatever she could to save the child, she wasn't ready to see if her vision would come true.

"Jinx is coming with us," Trigger told her, nodding toward the other man.

"What?" Alanna asked in confusion, glancing over at Jinx again. "Why?"

"Because you are pack, sweetheart. Jinx is pack."

She'd known he'd helped others in their pack before, along with members of RARE. She heard how he saved

Rikki's life when she would have died, guiding Angel through how to change her, making her a shifter like them. He'd helped get Storm back home after she was captured by the General. He'd removed a threat from Janie, allowing her to live free of the General as well. Alanna knew Jinx had been instrumental on several missions, even if she didn't have all the details.

Alanna could tell Trigger was happy to have the man go with them, but he couldn't feel the turmoil and despair coming off the warrior in waves. The heaviness that weighed him down from all his responsibilities. She could feel it all, and as much as she wanted his help, she didn't want to add to the burdens he was already struggling through.

"As much as I appreciate your willingness to help, I can't ask that of you," she whispered, unable to stop the sheen of tears in her eyes.

"You didn't ask." Jinx's voice was cold and unyielding, but his true feelings were anything but that.

"It's not up to you to save the entire world, Jinx."

Jinx pushed his chair back and stood. "I'm not trying to save the world, little bear. Just an important part of it." When she would have protested, he turned and walked away without another word.

"What was that all about?" Sharina asked softly, her eyes following him as he disappeared into the woods surrounding them.

"He's a wounded, tortured soul," Alanna replied, her eyes still on the trees. "He gives and gives to everyone and asks for nothing in return. A lone wolf, even if he doesn't necessarily want to be. A good man, one of the best, but he's lost."

"And the food?"

Alanna looked over at Trigger, finally allowing the tears she'd been holding back to slip out and down her face. "It isn't my place to tell, but from what I saw, he has every reason to not eat anything anyone else fixes for him, no matter who they are. That man has been through hell and back. He hides his true feelings behind a hard mask, but he feels things deeply." She paused, cocking her head to the side as she glanced back over at where Jinx had just been not too long ago. "I want to help him, Trigger."

"Then we will."

14

Trigger pulled onto Dominic Reeves' pack lands, following closely behind the vehicle in front of them that held four members of RARE, along with both Chase and Angel. The large SUV he was driving was second in line of a convoy of four. The others were packed with both RARE and Chase's elite enforcers. They had all come heavily armed and were ready to take out any threat. This meeting was supposed to be a cordial one, but they were all aware that could turn on them at any time.

The first vehicle stopped in front of a gorgeous two-story log cabin style house that they'd found out was considered the alpha house and was where Dominic lived with Parker and his parents. The rest of his pack was scattered over thousands of acres in small homes built by the pack themselves.

The rest of the convoy spread out to the right of the SUV facing the house, so they were all in a line, with a large space between each vehicle. It would give them more room to maneuver just in case they needed it. Trigger had no doubt they looked intimidating, a row of matching black SUVs with darkly tinted windows that had bullet proof glass. Chase and Angel took what they did seriously — the jobs the shifter council sent them on, along with mercenary missions RARE accepted. They spared no expense when it came to the necessities needed to do that job and do it well.

Trigger knew the third and fourth vehicles had slowed down a mile out just enough that Rikki and Charlotte could jump out. They would be somewhere near where no one could find them, their sniper rifles trained on the men in front of them. They would also be scanning for any other threats in the area. Trace was also somewhere with his own weapon, ready to join the party if needed.

A male stood on the large, wraparound porch, his arms crossed over his thick chest as he watched them arrive. He was tall, with long silver hair pulled back at the nape of his neck. His face was a blank mask, but even from where they sat, Trigger could see the intelligence in his dark gaze. His muscles bulged in the long-sleeved black shirt he wore, his thighs like tree trunks in his black jeans.

"Who's that?" Alanna asked from where she sat directly behind him in the middle seat, his mother next to her. He'd wanted her close, but not up front with him just in case things didn't go as planned and they needed to make an exit quickly before they even got out of the vehicle.

"That's Dante Reeves," Nico replied, his voice filled with satisfaction. "He's Dominic's father and is a member of the shifter council."

"What?" There was nervousness and fear in Alanna's one word question.

"Don't worry, sweetheart," Trigger said, meeting his mate's eyes in the rearview mirror. "Angel knows and respects Dante. She said there is no way in hell he would have gone along with whatever Dominic was planning. She knew he would be here, was counting on it actually. Their family is very close. There's no way Dante and his mate would stay away at a time like this."

Another man stepped out of the house and walked over to stand next to Dante. He mimicked Dante's stance, a hard set on his jaw. The two of them had similar features, but this man was younger, although not by much. He had a head full of dark hair sprinkled heavily with silver, that just touched his collar, the same dark eyes as Dante, and same build. Several weapons were visible on his body, along with a very lethal looking Katana strapped to his hip.

"And that one? Who is he?"

His mother's tone was quiet, but there was something in her tone that had Trigger turning to look at her. His eyes narrowed on the unusual paleness of her complexion and the tightness of her lips. Her gaze was on the second man, and the look in them had him frowning. There was apprehension, but also something else. Excitement?

"That's Dominic," Storm told them from where she and her mate, Steele, sat in the very back of the SUV. "I honestly don't understand what is going on with him. I've met him numerous times. He's a really good man. At least he was. I would never think him capable of what he has planned."

"People can do horrible things when trying to protect

the ones they love," Sharina said absently, her gaze never straying from Dominic. "He's in pain, afraid of losing his grandson. It has him making illogical choices. It doesn't make it right, but right now that man's world is falling apart."

Trigger was beginning to get a bad feeling in his gut about just who Dominic Reeves might be to his mother, but he kept quiet, hoping he was wrong.

"What are we waiting for?" Alanna asked, and Trigger hated the tremor he heard in her voice. He wanted to turn the vehicle around and get the hell out of there. Take his mate home and hide her away for the rest of their lives. It wouldn't be fair to her, but it didn't stop the deep need in him to want to protect her from every potential threat.

The loud rumble of a Harley grabbed his attention, and Trigger glanced out the back window to see Jinx making his way down the long lane to the house. He waited patiently for the man to stop next to them, put his kickstand down, and swing a leg over the bike.

"Nothing now," he said, shutting off their vehicle and removing his seatbelt. Glancing back, he glared at the women in the second row. "Do not, under any circumstances, open your doors until Nico and I open them for you. Do you understand?" They both nodded but kept quiet. "Steele and Storm will stay in here with you. Don't open the damn doors."

When he was sure they would comply, Trigger left the vehicle, shutting his door firmly behind him. He nodded to Jinx, and then walked next to the man to where Angel now waited at the bottom of the stairs next to her mate. Several members of RARE surrounded them, while the others spread out over the lawn with the White River Wolves elite enforcers.

Dante and Dominic moved in unison to stand at the edge of the porch right in front of them, not backing down from a possible confrontation. They were both strong, powerful men in their own right. Men you would want on your side if shit hit the fan. Not someone you wanted to go up against. Trigger hoped it didn't come to that.

Up close, he took in Dominic's exhausted, haggard appearance, and a part of him felt bad for the man. Another part of him wanted to grab the Katana from the bastard's hip and shove it into his conniving, manipulative heart.

"Dante. Dominic." Angel placed her hands lightly on her hips as she looked up at them.

"Angel." It was Dante who answered as his gaze swept over the number of men and women fanned out around the area. He lifted an eyebrow in question. "What can we do for you?"

"There's been some news brought to our attention recently that Chase and I agreed needed to be looked into," Angel said in a cold, hard voice, her eyes on Dominic.

"As much as I want to know what that is, I am unable to help right now." Dante's voice cracked slightly and he swallowed hard. "Our family is going through something, and I am needed here."

"I believe we are here for the same reason you are, Dante," Angel said somberly.

"What?"

"Six months ago, you sent us on an assignment to

rescue a bear." Chase glanced back at him, and Trigger gave him a nod to continue. "Dominic showed up on my land while I was gone. He first tried to get my enforcers to hand over Alanna to him by insinuating he was a council enforcer. Luckily, my mate was there and knew that wasn't the truth. Then, he tried to get Angel to give Alanna to him. Told her he needed the bear but refused to tell her why."

Dante had stiffened the second Chase mentioned the bear they rescued. When they said Dominic's name, his gaze went to his son.

"Technically, he shouldn't have even known about her," Angel cut in, a hard edge in her voice. "We can only assume that classified information came from you, Dante."

A pained expression crossed Dante's face as he looked back over at them. "Yeah," he said hoarsely. "That would be a good assumption." He shook his head. "I shouldn't have told anyone about her, not even Dominic."

"No, you shouldn't have." Angel's tone was low, deadly.

Dante's eyes lit with fire as he glared over at his son. "What the hell were you thinking, Dominic? That bear is not only under the protection of the White River Wolves, but also the council."

"I was thinking that my grandson is dying!" Dominic roared, slamming his hand down on the wooden railing next to him, causing a loud crack to fill the air as it splintered. "That my son and his wife will be devastated. That I am going to lose the brightest part of my life!"

"Dominic..."

"It doesn't matter," Dominic said bitterly, raking a hand through his thick hair.

"It does when you were planning on kidnapping her and making her heal Parker," Angel snapped. "Which could have killed her in the process. What she does, the gift she has, sucks the life right out of her Dominic. It could very well end her life."

"I would never have made her do anything." A tortured look ran across Dominic's face and he shook his head. "Yeah, I was planning on taking her from your land and bringing her here. But I would never have made her heal Parker. I would have asked her, but never forced her." He sucked in a ragged breath. "I just wanted to ask."

Trigger stepped forward, clearing his throat. With all eyes on him, he addressed Dominic directly. "You would have asked, and she would have given you what you need, because that is how my mate is. She has a heart bigger than anyone I've ever met. She wouldn't have been able to say no to a child in need, and she would have died because of it." He held up a hand when Dominic started to interrupt. "Alanna still wants to help you. She feels like it's her calling to help others, and I fully support her, but we are going to do this under my rules and supervision. With my alpha, alpha mate, mother, and Jinx in the room with us. If I think at any moment my mate is in danger, I will pull her out. I am in charge here, not you. If you don't agree, we will leave. It's as simple as that."

"She'll help?" Dominic asked, his brow furrowing in confusion. "But you said it will kill her."

"I also said I will pull her out if I think it is getting to that point. But then, after some time, we will try again. My bear is very stubborn and she will always put a child's life before her own. It's my job to make sure she survives."

Fuck, he hated this. As much as he wanted to help little Parker, he was worried about Alanna. He was going to have to watch her very closely, because he couldn't lose her.

"We agree," Dominic said hoarsely, his face lighting with hope. "Whatever you want, whatever you need, we agree. I'll give you anything."

Trigger watched him closely for a moment, then turned back to look at Jinx. The wolf sent him a small nod and walked over to the SUV. Opening the door, he leaned into the vehicle and said something no one else could hear, and then took a step back, holding out his hand. A small hand grasped it, and then Alanna slid out of the SUV. Jinx guided her over to Trigger, placing her hand in his before taking a step back.

"No," Alanna whispered, her eyes going back to Jinx. "Please, stay with us."

"I'm not going anywhere, little bear," Jinx promised quietly, coming back up beside her. "I'll be with you and your mate the entire time." He looked up at Dominic, and raised his voice slightly, a deadly edge to it. "Phoenix and Jaxson will come in with us also. Alanna trusts them explicitly. Aiden and Xavier will stand just outside the door of the room. My father and his mate will also be in the house with us."

"I don't give a damn who is in the house, as long as..." Dominic's voice trailed off when the door on the other side of the SUV slammed shut and Trigger's mother appeared.

The tigress held her head high as she walked forward and stood beside Trigger. There was no doubt in his mind who Dominic was to his mother now. Not when he saw the stunned look in the alpha's eyes after he inhaled deeply, drawing in Sharina's scent.

"Where is the child?" Sharina asked, her stare locked with Dominic's.

Before he could answer, the door behind them opened, and another man stepped out onto the porch. This one was a lot younger than both Dante and Dominic. From the extensive research Jaxson had completed, Trigger knew this was Derek, Parker's father. He was just thirty-five years old, and his young wife Ami twenty-six. Derek's face was ravaged with pain, a trail of tears on his cheeks. "Dad? Grandfather? I need you. It's time."

"Time?"

"Parker is..." he let out a harsh sob, before continuing. "The healer said there is nothing more that can be done. The Gods are coming for him."

"The hell they are," Sharina snarled, leaving Trigger's side and stalking up the stairs. "They've taken enough from me. They are not taking my new grandchild too!"

The man's eyes widened in shock, his gaze swinging to Dominic and then back to Sharina. That same hope that had shown in Dominic just moments before began to light in Parker's father's eyes. Sharina reached out a hand to him and he took it, then she turned back to Alanna and did the same. "Come daughter of mine, let's go meet your nephew. He needs us."

Holy hell, his mother was amazing. She looked so regal, like a queen. Or the alpha mate she was now.

As Trigger and Jinx followed close behind Alanna and Sharina, the worry he felt before came back full force. What if something happened and he couldn't pull Alanna back using the mate bond? What if he lost control of the situation, and in doing so let her go further than he should? What if he lost her?

Don't worry. I've got her.

He didn't even flinch when the words flowed through his mind. He recognized Jinx's voice immediately and had no problem with the wolf being inside his head. Not when his mate's life was on the line.

What if something goes wrong?

It won't.

How can you be sure?

Because I'm going in with her, Jinx said confidently.

What? You can do that?

Yep. Hold on.

Trigger kept walking down a long hallway, then up a flight of stairs to the second floor. They were almost to the room where he knew the child was, the scent of the sickness heavy in the air, when he heard Jinx's voice again.

Phoenix and Jaxson are going to watch us all closely. They will guard me, while you, Chase and Angel guard your mate. Dad and Storm will check out the house and make sure there are no possible threats near. Aiden and Xavier will stay by the door to make sure no one else tries to enter.

Trigger took a deep breath and let it out slowly. It was time. He had a mate to protect while she fought to save a child. He would not let her down.

Let's do this.

15

Alanna's heart pounded loudly in her chest as she entered the little boy's room. She passed a woman who stood just to the right of the door, brushing away tears that flowed unchecked down her cheeks. Parker's mother, Ami, was by the window, her arms wrapped tightly around her waist. Her shoulders were hunched over, and her body shook with silent sobs. An older woman stood next to her, a look of utter defeat on her face. She had to be the pack healer, which meant the first woman was Dante's mate.

Ami and the healer turned to look at Alanna, and then behind her at the rest of the people that filed into the bedroom. Derek immediately went to his wife and put an arm around her, pulling her close. Lowering his head, he spoke quietly to her in a soft soothing tone.

"What's happening?" the healer demanded, her eyes narrowing on Alanna.

"They've come to help," Dominic told her, his voice rough with worry.

"What? How?"

Alanna ignored them as she quickly crossed the room to where Parker lay in a twin bed that looked as if it had been lovingly carved by hand. His small, still body was under a dark blue comforter covered with beautiful gray wolves, a bright moon up in one corner. He held a stuffed dark gray wolf to his chest. It would seem he'd embraced the shifter life, even if he was human himself. Although, that could change someday if he found a shifter mate.

Sitting on the edge of the bed, Alanna took the child's hand in hers. Tuning out everything around her, she leaned down and rested her cheek next to his, gently tracing her fingers lightly down his arm. She could hear the faint beat of his heart and his small chest rose and fell, but just barely. The healer was right. After a long drawn-out battle, Parker was giving up his fight.

That was unacceptable. She'd come here to save him, and that was what she was going to do. She would fight for him if he was unable to fight for himself.

Hey, little man, Alanna whispered softly, sending the words floating through his mind. *My name is Alanna. I'm so sorry it took me as long as it did to come to you, but I'm here now.* There was a small stutter in his breathing, then nothing. Slowly, she let herself merge with him and couldn't stop the small cry that slipped out at what she encountered.

Agonizing pain throughout his entire body. As if the cancer was literally eating at him, which it was. Confusion. Loss. Despair. Horrible fear. His will to live was almost gone. He wanted to move on, where he wouldn't feel the way he'd been feeling for the past year since they found the cancer. Sick, tired, nauseous. Constantly hurting.

Slowly, Alanna started siphoning the pain from him, sucking it into her body, knowing she needed to take it from him so he could find the will to fight again. *Give me your pain, my nephew. Let me take it, shoulder it for you so you can renew your fight to live. Let me help you, little prince.*

Tired. Hurts.

Alanna startled when she heard Parker's voice, a small gasp of surprise slipping past her lips. No one had ever responded to her when she'd talked to them using telepathy while healing them before. Was he gifted?

I know it does, little prince, but I promise you it will get better. I'm fighting for you, but I need your help. Can you do that for me?

He didn't answer her right away, but finally she heard him say in a faint, weak voice, *I can try.*

"That's all I can ask for, little prince. You try, and I will do the rest."

Alanna was unaware she'd answered Parker out loud, and she didn't see the look of shock on the faces in the room. She kept pulling the terrible pain from his small, ravaged body, drawing it into hers. It was beginning to hurt so much and she struggled to block out the agony. If this child had lived with it for months, then she could for a few weeks. This was going to have her down for longer than she'd ever been before, but not helping the boy wasn't even an option.

I'm scared.

I know you are, buddy. I am too. But you know what?

What.

His voice was so soft now, she was afraid he was drifting too far away and she wouldn't be able to hold him to her.

We have our own guardians who are fighting with us. Fighting for you to live. To stay here with your daddy and mommy and Grandpa Dominic.

Papa.

Sweat beaded up on her forehead as Alanna kept up the steady flow of pulling the pain and agony from him. As she did, she also started to remove the cancer, absorbing the disease into herself, while flooding him with her healing power.

"Yes, little prince, your papa. He's the reason I'm here. He came to my alpha mate and asked for help, for you."

She was once again unaware she was speaking out loud. For some reason, she was having trouble concentrating. The pain she was absorbing was hitting her so much quicker than it had in the past, and she'd never dealt with a disease like cancer before. It was spreading through her like fire, and as much as she tried to ignore it, she was beginning to struggle. It was hard to focus on what she was doing and to keep up with taking in the child's pain and disease while pushing healing power his way.

Love Papa.

"Your Papa loves you too, buddy. So much."

"Oh, Gods." Dominic's groan of misery reached her, but she steeled herself against it. Parker's pain was what she needed to focus on. No one else's, not right now.

Suddenly, Alanna was aware of another presence slipping into her mind gently, but also full of determination and resolve. Slowly the confusion she'd been feeling began to recede as she felt a deep strength and intense power being shared with her. She knew exactly who it was coming from, and a soft smile tilted up the corners of her lips.

Thank you, Jinx.

At first there was no reply, and then she heard *I told you I would be here, little bear.*

Yes, he had. As much as she hadn't wanted to use him like so many other people in his life, she couldn't deny how happy she was that he was there with her. For once, she wasn't alone in her quest to heal.

I need to lay down, Jinx, she whispered. *I need you to position Parker so his heart is next to mine. I've been slowly taking some of the cancer from him as I take his pain, but I need to concentrate on getting rid of the cancer attacking his heart and lungs so he has the will to fight. It will help if our hearts are lined up when I do it.*

Got it.

She heard Jinx say something aloud, and then she was being lifted and placed on the bed next to Parker, lying on her side. The little boy was turned, so they were chest to chest, his heart resting against hers. The comforter was pulled up over them both as she snuggled the boy close.

Guardians?

Parker's voice was slightly stronger. Not by much, but enough for her to see he was willing to try. That he wanted to live.

Alanna smiled a sweet, tender smile as she whispered, "Oh, yes, our guardians. I'm sorry, little prince. I got sidetracked." She was once again speaking out loud, but this time it was on purpose. She wanted to share with his family, let them be a part of what was happening. It was something she could give them when she knew they were filled with terror. "My guardian is a big bad scary Siberian tiger. He watches out for me and keeps me safe when the darkness comes for me."

Darkness?

She was concentrating on his heart, removing all of the cancer she could find. It was going quicker than she'd thought it would, and soon she'd be able to switch to his lungs.

"Yes. You know how you are struggling against the disease in your body right now? Well, later I will be struggling against what I call the darkness. It always wants to pull me down into it and hold me there, to crush me, but my tiger will be there for me and will help me fight all of my demons."

Strong.

"Oh yes. He's very strong and so fierce. Trust me, the darkness doesn't stand a chance against my tiger."

"Damn straight, mate." At the sound of Trigger's voice, a part of her reached for him and a soft gasp slipped out when she felt a small tug on their mate bond. Not only was he there, but she could feel him. Feel the tie between them and the way their souls were merged together.

Done with Parker's heart, happy to hear that it was beating louder and stronger, she moved to his lungs.

For some reason, what she was doing now seemed somehow easier than in the past. It was still hard on her, still wearing her out, but not to the degree it had before. She knew part of it was Jinx, but she had a strong suspicion it was because of the bond between mates as well.

My guardian?

"Yes, your guardian. He's as fierce as my tiger. A powerful wolf, who has more strength and courage than anyone I've ever met before. He will fight for you, and keep you safe, little prince. He's here with us now. Can you feel him?"

She felt Jinx stir in her mind, felt his surprise at being named the child's guardian before he masked his reaction to the words.

He's here?

Right here, little man.

Your name?

There was a slight hesitation. *Jinx.*

"Jinx."

Someone let out a shocked gasp when Parker spoke aloud for the first time since they'd arrived. It was a whisper, but everyone in the room heard it.

"He hasn't talked in days," Parker's father said into the stunned silence. "He tried but couldn't get any words out."

Yes, Jinx.

Keep me safe?

Jinx leaned over and ran a hand over the boy's hair. "Yeah, buddy, I'll keep you safe. That's what guardians do."

Alanna was moving swiftly, removing the cancer from Parker's lungs. She was so close to being done, but even with Jinx's help, she was starting to weaken.

Protect.

"Yes, you are under my protection," Jinx replied gruffly.

Alanna realized Jinx was talking aloud now, and she vaguely wondered if it was so Parker's family could be a part of the conversation, the way she'd tried to include them.

Today?

"I am your guardian now, Parker Reeves, as Alanna said. That means I will always protect you. You need me, I will be there."

Alanna's brow wrinkled at the words. Had she just inadvertently placed another responsibility onto the wolf's shoulders? He had so much to bear already, he didn't need more.

It was my choice, Alanna. Not yours.

But...

No. My choice. One I gladly take on.

Alanna sighed deeply, closing her eyes. She would have to take Jinx at his word, because she was beginning to fight an exhaustion that was starting to seep into every bone in her body. Parker's lungs and heart were clear, as was his throat. She could feel Jinx tiring as well, and knew she needed to remove the rest of the cancer quickly before she couldn't hold the merge anymore.

Head.

Alanna paused at the pained whisper, and the dark pain in the child's voice. It wasn't that he hadn't been hurting this entire time, but something was different about the way he said that one word. Something was off.

"Jinx." She was asking for help because her struggle was getting worse. She hadn't made it to the boy's head yet. It had been where she was planning on going next. And then doing a sweep down his body to remove what was left of the disease.

I've got you, little bear.

She felt Jinx's hand on her shoulder, felt more power being pushed into her. She accepted it gratefully, needing all the strength she could get.

"Mate," she gasped, needing to know Trigger was with her too.

"I've got you, Alanna."

She felt her mate's hand on her other shoulder, lending his strength as well. His love and determination flowed through the mate bond, and she was so glad they'd taken the step to forge that bond before attempting to save Parker.

Raising a hand, Alanna gently set it on the back of the child's head, and then leaned down until her forehead rested against his. He whimpered softly and her heart caught in her chest. Then he cried out, a sob of agony that pulled tears from her eyes. A sound that told of his suffering.

"Derek, please." It was Parker's mother, her voice trembling with emotion. "I can't handle hearing him like this. He's in so much pain."

"Let her do what she needs to do," Angel said quietly. "Trust me, he's in pain now, but it won't last."

Derek began whispering soft words to his mate, but Alanna tuned them out. Slowly, she let herself slide into Parker's mind, aware that Jinx was with her the entire time. Suddenly, extreme agony pierced through her, and her own head felt as if it were engulfed in fiery pain. It was as if the cancer was concentrating on one specific part in his frontal lobe, attacking it, doing whatever it could to hurt him. To kill him.

She was unaware of the muffled scream that tore from her throat, or the tears that began to flow down her face. She didn't pull away, she couldn't. Whatever he was going through was now for her to endure as well. She refused to let him suffer alone.

I'm right here, little bear. You can do this. Relieve him of this torture, and then we will all rest.

Jinx was right. It was time to get this done. She wouldn't last much longer, and leaving Parker to face something like this alone wasn't an option. Not if she could help it. She had to remove everything, and she had to do it now.

Concentrating on the place that was hurting him the worst, Alanna began to draw the pain into her. Her entire body was shaking. Sweat coated her skin, dripping down her temples and over her chest. She could feel Jinx with her and knew without his help there was no way she would still be conscious. She would have lost her hold to reality a long time ago.

"You're doing great, baby."

Her mate, her love, her life. He was there. Encouraging her, holding her to him with their bond, somehow sending reassurance and love through it. And there was pride; so much pride. He was proud of her and what she was doing, even if he was terrified. That emotion was there too.

It's going away.

Parker's words vaguely registered, and a small smile slipped over her lips. She was glad he was starting to feel less pain.

It's time to pull back, little bear. You've taken most of his pain away, along with the majority of the cancer. We need to come back and finish this another day.

Alanna ignored the voice. She knew it was Jinx, knew she was supposed to listen to him when he gave the word to pull back, but she couldn't. Parker had lived in pain for so long. He deserved to be free of it. Free of the cancer.

Free to grow and live his life to the fullest. She was going to take all of it from him now. He wasn't going to have to wait one more day.

Alanna, I said to pull back. Now.

No, Jinx. I can do this.

She moved through Parker's head, taking with her every last bit of the disease she could find, not wanting to leave anything behind that might decide to start growing again. Then she moved down to do a final sweep through his body. The cancer had mostly been centered on his heart, lungs, and brain. While it was everywhere, the rest of it was easier to find and destroy. Or, she would have considered it easier if she wasn't at the end of her endurance.

Her head was throbbing, soft moans coming from deep in her throat. Blinding pain streaked up her spine and into her head. Silent screams erupted in her mind, ones she fought to keep from everyone else. It was a losing battle, and soon the room was filled with her screams.

"What is it? What's happening?"

The terror in Mama's voice penetrated the darkness she was fighting against. Alanna tried to open her mouth. Tried to tell her everything was going to be okay. But she couldn't speak. Couldn't open her eyes. Couldn't move.

It's gone. The pain, it's all going. I don't hurt anymore.

She wanted to respond to the child's words but couldn't. She didn't have the energy. She made one last sweep through Parker's body, making sure she had removed all the cancer, along with all the boy's pain. It was slow going. She was sluggish, exhausted, and in agony like she'd never felt before.

It's gone now, little bear. Time to come back to us.

Alanna wanted that, wanted it so badly, but found she had no idea how to make it happen. She was lost, the darkness taking over. She'd never had that happen while she was still merged with someone she'd healed, and wondered belatedly what it might do to her. Would she survive?

"Dammit, Alanna, sever your connection with Parker. Now!"

Jinx was loud, demanding, wanting her to do something. She couldn't understand what. Someone was whimpering, crying, screaming in pain. She wanted to help whomever it was but couldn't move. Couldn't seem to function at all.

"Trigger, you need to help me get your mate out of there."

Trigger. Her mate. Her love. Her everything.

"Shit! What do I do?"

"Hold tight to your bond. Yank on it. I don't know. Pull her the fuck out!"

Jinx sounded so upset. She'd never heard him like that before. She didn't like it. He was a good man. One of the best. He should be happy. Should be with his family. With his pack. With them.

Alanna began to shiver uncontrollably. She was so cold. Ice cold.

"Alanna? Alanna, daughter! Don't you leave me. Oh God, don't leave me. Please don't leave me!"

She felt someone's terror, their hopelessness and despair. Pain. It was flowing to her, from them to her. There was also love. So much love.

"Come back to me, mate. Please, don't leave me. Choose to live. Choose me."

She knew it was her tiger, but she couldn't respond. Of course, she would choose him. She would always choose him. He should know that.

Someone was taking something from her, pulling it from her arms. Then she heard a small voice ask, "What's wrong with her?"

Parker. He was alive and talking. She wanted to smile at that, but couldn't seem to make her facial muscles do what she wanted.

"We do it together, Trigger. You concentrate on the mate bond, do what you can to pull her out while I push her out."

"Got it."

"In three, two, one, now!"

She felt a tug in her chest, then a harder one. And something was pushing her, shoving her hard. She was so confused, so lost.

It is not your time, sweet bear.

Not her time?

No, it isn't your time. You have a long life to live. With your mate, your new family, and I see some cubs in your future.

Cubs?

There was soft laughter. *Yes, little one, cubs. You have served us well, saving several important lives, but now you need to fight to save one of the most important ones. Your own.*

Goddess?

Yes, child.

Want that. Want my mate and cubs.

There was more soft laughter, and then, *Fight for them,*

Alanna. Your future awaits you. You just have to reach out and grab it.

The presence was gone as quickly as it had appeared. But when she felt that tug in her chest again, she did what the Goddess said and reached for it. Embraced it.

"Come to me, baby. That's right, just like that."

Alanna felt herself leave whatever hell she'd been in, a place caught between Parker's mind and body and her own. A place she was afraid she was going to be lost in forever.

"Alanna? Are you okay, Alanna?" It was Parker. Sweet, kind, Parker. She'd seen his soul when she'd been merged with him and knew he would be a good man someday.

"She'll be okay." Trigger sounded so sure of that, that even though she felt like she was in the fiery pits of hell, suffering through a pain like no other, she believed him.

"How do you know?"

"Because, buddy, I'm her guardian. Remember? It's my job to take care of her; one I take very seriously."

"Her tiger!" She wanted to smile at the excitement in the boy's voice. It was so good to hear him happy and pain free.

"Yes, I'm hers."

"We need to go," Jinx cut in. "We have to get Alanna home."

"What? You aren't staying?" That was Dominic. "I have several rooms you can all use. We can take care of her here."

"We will take my daughter home where she will be most comfortable."

Wait? That wasn't right. Sharina was supposed to stay here, wasn't she?

Alanna moaned in confusion, knowing she was forgetting something. But she couldn't concentrate on anything now. She was done. She let herself slip away into unconsciousness, knowing the darkness would be reaching for her as soon as she woke again, but this time she wasn't afraid. Her mate would be there. Her guardian. He would keep her safe.

16

Alanna sat in the patio chair, wrapped in a large, dark blue fleece blanket. She wore a pair of jeans, a heavy sweatshirt, and wool socks with a pair of tennis shoes on her feet. Her long, brown hair hung in a thick braid down her back, her eyes watchful as she cupped a mug of hot chocolate in her hand. Whipped cream, marshmallows, and a sprinkle of chocolate chips over the top; just the way she liked it.

"Are you sure you're warm enough, mate?"

She glanced over at Trigger, the love she felt for him shining in her eyes and overflowing in her heart. He'd stayed by her side the entire three weeks she'd been down, stuck in the darkness, fighting her way out. This time, he let visitors stop by and talk to her, and he allowed Doc Josie to check on her daily. Fallon came by every morning, but she never stayed long. Alanna was worried about her. She was a good friend, but it felt as if she were pulling back, trying to create a distance between them. It was something she would need to address in the future, but Alanna chose to let it go for now.

She was surprised it had only been three weeks that she was under this time, but was sure it had something to do with Jinx. Somehow, his being with her throughout the healing, sharing his power the way he did, had helped her. It might also have had something to do with the mate bond. Even in the darkness, she'd felt the link. The slight tug, tying her to Trigger, allowing her to feel his love and support.

"Alanna?"

Alanna winced when she realized she hadn't answered him yet. "Sorry. Yes, I'm good."

"We can go inside and wait."

"No, he'll be here soon."

"Are you waiting for me, little bear?"

A wide smile immediately appeared, and Alanna rose. Setting her mug down, she quickly crossed to Jinx and wrapped her arms tightly around his waist. He stiffened at first, then she felt his arms slowly close around her and he held her to him. They stood like that for several minutes before she finally moved back, giving him another, smaller smile. "I knew you'd come today."

His grin was slow in coming, but when it did, she caught her breath. The man was going to stop some girl's heart someday. "I've been by a couple of times to check on you."

Alanna nodded, knowing what he said was true, then turned to go reclaim her chair. Trigger reached over and retrieved her hot chocolate, handing it to her. "Your shivering, mate. Drink some of this."

She didn't argue because he was right. She was cold.

But she knew how much Jinx hated to be indoors, so she'd talked Trigger into waiting for him on the back porch.

"I'll be quick," Jinx said, as if he knew the real reason they were outside, and it wasn't to enjoy the weather and hot chocolate. He probably did. She was sure the man had more gifts than she did. "Chase told me how you came to live with the White River Wolves, Alanna."

"He did?"

"Yes. I admit, I asked him. I wanted to know what brought you here, but I didn't want to be rude and take the answer from your mind."

She cocked her head to the side, looking closely at the wolf. "Thank you, Jinx. But just so you know, you have my permission to look for answers if you ever need them. I have nothing to hide, and after what we've been through together, I trust you more than I trust anyone else, except for Trigger."

When he glanced over at Trigger, as if seeking his permission, her mate gave him a nod. "That goes for me too, Jinx. For both of us."

Jinx regarded them quietly, then walked over to grab one of the patio chairs, placing it in front of Alanna. He sat down and leaned forward, holding his hands out. She smiled, and didn't hesitate to put her hands in his, even though it did surprise her a little. She knew he didn't care for other people to touch him, any more than he cared for being inside unfamiliar places. Or to just be inside at all.

"If I initiate the touch, it's different." Her eyes sprang from where his much larger hands were holding her tiny ones to meet his deep brown gaze.

"I'm sorry, Jinx. I don't go looking for other people's secrets. They just find me sometimes."

He shrugged, squeezing her hands lightly. "You are a better person than me, Alanna. Because normally, I do go looking." He hesitated for a moment before glancing over at Trigger, including him in the conversation. "I took a quick trip a couple of days ago. To North Carolina." When Alanna stiffened, he held her hands a bit tighter. "Your brother will no longer be a threat to you, little bear."

Alanna's eyes roamed over his face, taking in the hard set of his jawline and the slightly cold look in his eyes. She thought she understood what he was telling her but wanted to make sure. "To me, or to anyone?"

"To anyone," Jinx confirmed shortly. "I can show you if you would like? So, you know it to be true."

Alanna slowly shook her head, a feeling of peace settling in her chest. "No, Jinx, you don't need to show me. I appreciate the offer, but I know you would never lie to me."

I want to help him now.

Are you sure, mate? Are you up to it?

She turned to look at Trigger, a soft smile on her lips. "Yes, I'm sure. I'm ready."

Trigger nodded, and they both looked over at Jinx. "You went with us to help Parker, Jinx. You said it was because that is what pack does." Jinx frowned slightly but kept quiet. "You also just removed a very real threat to Alanna's life. I'm assuming you will also say it is because that is what pack does."

"It is." Jinx shrugged, his gaze leaving them to look out toward the trees surrounding them before coming back again. "That's what my dad says. And I've watched Chase and some of the other pack members. They all take care of each other. I know I'm not technically a part of your pack, but Chase says I will be someday when I'm ready."

"That's where you're wrong," Trigger interjected. "You already *are* pack, Jinx. And you have given us two very important gifts. First by keeping my mate alive when she saved Parker's life." He held up his hand when Jinx looked as if he were going to say something. "Don't deny it. We both know she would have died if you weren't there, sharing your power with her. Helping me pull her out at the end. She would have died, which means I would have chosen to follow. Because of you, we are both still here today. And don't think that I don't know the toll it took on you. You may have left right when we got back home, but I saw you. If I thought you would have stayed, I would have put you in the guest room and watched over you myself."

"It was my honor," Jinx finally said, accepting what Trigger was telling him.

"Eliminating the threat of Doug was the second gift you've given us. There is no doubt in my mind that he would have come for Alanna. He would have come, and he would have failed, but there is always a chance she could have been hurt."

Jinx gave them a short nod.

"Now, my mate would like to give you a gift in return. Because it is what pack does, but also because she and I both consider you a friend, Jinx. Please, accept this gift from her. From us."

Jinx hesitated, looking at them in confusion before he slowly nodded again.

Alanna didn't waste any time. She'd wanted his permission, and she'd just received it. Now, she was going to help him before he had time to change his mind. Holding his hands tightly in hers, she closed her eyes and reached for him, letting that part of her out that allowed her to feel the emotions of those around her. She'd never actually tried to seek out emotions the way she was with Jinx, but she found it easy to make the connection since she was touching him.

First, she sought out the nervousness and anxiety he experienced every time he had to enter a place he had no desire to go. She found it quickly, since they were sitting so near the cottage and he was worried she might want to go inside because of the cold. She started pulling those feelings from him and into her before she searched for the terror he felt when he was expected to eat what others made. That was also easy to find, considering they'd set an extra mug of hot chocolate on the table just in case he wanted one after this was all over.

While she was taking all of that from him, absorbing it into herself, she found another fear. One that he would never be able to be what everyone expected him to be. A brother, a son, a guardian, a savior... a friend.

Jinx tried to pull away from her, but Alanna held on tightly. "Please Jinx, let me do this for you. Please."

She felt the shudder that ran through his body, making his hands shake slightly, but he stayed where he was.

"I don't want to hurt you," he said hoarsely.

Alanna opened her eyes and slowly raised her head to meet his now bright emerald gaze. "You won't. I promise. This doesn't affect me the way healing someone physically does. I won't be in pain. I won't go into the darkness."

It was all true. He wouldn't scent any lies. She wasn't

going to tell him that she would feel all the negative emotions she was drawing from him for days. She'd only done it the one time, with Sharina, so she really had no idea how long it would last. But she didn't care. She and Trigger had talked extensively about it, and they both agreed that after everything the man had done for them, they wanted to help Jinx.

Focusing her attention back on her main goal, Alanna closed her eyes again. There was resentment toward the General, a man who was now dead. Definitely a feeling Jinx didn't need to be hauling around with him anymore. Frustration that he was unable to find the head of the faction that Ebony was working for. Anger for both the General and Ebony for making him live a life he hated. Sorrow for all the people being held captive by first the General, and now Ebony. Especially Amber, one of the General's daughters.

Alanna's heart stuttered when she saw exactly who Amber was. She might have been daughter to one of the most evil men who ever lived, but she was so different than him. Sweet, kind, and caring. She'd helped those captives Jinx worried about, saving several of them. She was mate to Bane, one of the members of RARE. And she was gone, taken by Ebony and hidden somewhere even Jinx was unable to find her. Bane and his sister Sapphire were looking for her, but there were no leads. Jinx had so much rage, sadness, and guilt in him from that one thing alone. She refused to allow him to feel the way he was. She took it all. Every last horrible emotion associated with a woman who no one could find.

Finally, when she was sure she'd done as much as she

could, Alanna opened her eyes and swayed slightly in her chair before leaning back against it.

"What did you do?" Jinx asked in awe, slowly pulling his hands from hers and sitting back in his own seat. "I feel different. Lighter somehow."

Alanna reached for Trigger, needing his touch, but kept her gaze on Jinx. "You know how I can heal a body physically?" Jinx nodded. "Well, I learned a few weeks ago that I can," she paused, unsure how to say it. "Well, I can heal emotions too." When he frowned, she tried again. "I took a lot of your negative emotions from you. Or maybe think of it as negative energy. Your anxiety, fear, rage, sorrow, guilt. I left you some of the anger, because I feel like you will need it to push forward on the journey you are following, but not too much."

"I've never heard of an ability like that before."

"Me neither," Alanna admitted. "I was actually shocked when it happened with Sharina. But she was hurting so much, I just let it follow the course it wanted to."

"Before Alanna healed my mother, she wouldn't even leave the house. We lost our streak in a raid by a group of humans who hunted shifters. We watched them murder my grandparents and my father. When Chase found us and brought us here, things were better for her until I left for the military." There was sadness in Trigger's gaze when he related the story, but Alanna was proud of him for telling Jinx. He hadn't told many people, and she believed it would help him to talk about it. "My mother started refusing to leave the house. She was filled with so much anxiety, sadness, rage." He glanced over at her, and brought her hand up to his lips, feathering a kiss across her knuckles. "My mate took all of that from her. Brought her peace. Gave her back her life."

Jinx swallowed hard, his gaze going to the third cup on the table, and then over to the door to their home.

"We will never push you to do anything, Jinx," she said softly, "but if you try, I think you will find your fears are lessened now. That terror that held you back from trusting anyone after what happened to you isn't there anymore. I won't say you will automatically learn to trust, but the fear holding you back won't be the oppressive weight it was before."

Slowly, Jinx reached over to grip the handle on the cup of hot chocolate, bringing it to his lips. He looked her in the eyes as he took a small sip, then a bigger one. She laughed when he pulled the mug back and there was a mustache of whip cream on his top lip.

"Wow. That's good."

Alanna laughed again as she nodded in agreement. "It's the marshmallows and chocolate chips on top. It makes all the difference."

17

Trigger watched Jinx walk away, the wolf's step a little lighter, his shoulders a little looser. The man still held the weight of the world on them, but without all the negative emotions bombarding him, he was better equipped to handle his responsibilities.

He gathered up his and Jinx's mugs, and followed Alanna into the house, his mind on one thing only. He slipped up behind his mate, his front pressed to her back. Setting the mugs he held in the sink in front of her, he lowered his head, placing his mouth over the mark he'd given her, claiming her as his. He scraped it with his fangs, loving the shiver that ran through her body.

Sliding his hands under her sweatshirt, he grasped both it and the little pink tee shirt she wore and tugged them up and off. His hands went to the clasp of her bra, and he slipped the three little prongs free and slid the purple lace over her shoulders and down her arms, letting it fall to the floor. Quickly, he rid himself of his own shirt and sweatshirt, wanting nothing between them. He toed off his shoes, and undid the snap on his pants, shoving them down and off, taking his black boxer briefs with them.

Then he switched his full attention back to his mate.

"You are so beautiful, baby. So damn beautiful." Trigger ran his hands over the smooth, silky skin on her back, down to the jeans she wore that cupped her sexy ass just right. He reached around and undid the button and slid his hands over the waistband of her jeans. Grasping them, he pushed them down. Kneeling, he lifted first one foot, removing her shoe, sock, and pant leg, and then did the other.

Alanna whimpered softly, a needy sound that had his cock so damn hard it hurt. He ran his palms over the soft, light purple satin that covered her milky white flesh, leaning in to nip at the skin at the curve of her ass. She cried out, pushing back into him, clutching tightly to the counter. He nipped at the other side, giving it the same attention, and she let out a low, breathless moan.

"Turn around, mate." He could smell her excitement, the scent driving him wild. He wanted to taste her.

She turned and he wasted no time sliding the small slip of lacey satin down her legs and off. Then his mouth was on her, his hands gripping her hips, his tongue sliding through her lips. He growled as her taste filled his mouth, his cock pulsing, wanting inside her.

"Trigger! Oh God, please!"

He shoved his tongue inside her, his growls intensifying, deep and loud. He was so fucking hard. Trigger licked through her lips and found that small, hard bundle of nerves. He licked and sucked, eating at her as he slid two fingers into her wet channel. Alanna's hands went to his hair, grasping tightly to the thick strands as she rocked against him. Soon, she was screaming as she flew apart on his tongue.

Trigger rose and pulled her against him, cupping her ass in his hands. Lifting her up, he groaned when she wrapped her legs around him, placing her mound tight against his cock. He moved over so he could rest her back against the wall and reached down to guide his hard, straining dick into her hot sheath. She was wet and so fucking tight it felt as if she were strangling his cock. He pushed slowly inside until he bottomed out, his balls resting against the curve of her ass.

"Trigger!"

Trigger slammed his mouth onto hers, the kiss hard and demanding. He'd only taken her once since she'd recovered from healing Parker, and that time it was slow, sweet, and sensual. This was going to be fast, hard, and downright dirty. He needed his mate.

One hand was underneath her ass holding her in place, the other found her breast, and he lowered his head to nip at the hard, pink nipple. Alanna cried out, bucking against him, raking her nails down his back.

He snarled around her breast, biting down on the turgid nipple as he pulled his hips back, sliding halfway out of her, and then thrust back in. He didn't hold back, taking her hard and fast, pounding into her as he nipped at the flesh on first one breast, then the other, loving the marks he left on her. His marks.

Alanna grasped his shoulders tightly, her nails digging into his skin. Her head fell back against the wall, her mouth open as she panted and moaned with little sexy growls mixed in. The sounds she was making were driving him crazy, and he knew he wasn't going to last long.

Trigger lowered his hand between them and found her clit, rubbing it with his thumb. He thrust harder, faster, chasing his orgasm. When he felt her channel tighten around him, squeezing his cock hard, he lowered his head to her neck and came with a grunt. Finding the mark he left on her weeks before, he sank his teeth deep. It was a claiming, something he would do every single time he took her because she was his.

Alanna's fangs bit into his shoulder, and he removed his own teeth and threw his head back, coming again with a loud shout. He continued to move his hips, plunging in and out of her, until he was finally spent.

"How about we find our bed and do that again?" he asked, leaning down to capture one of her nipples while he rolled the other one in between his thumb and forefinger.

His mate's sweet laughter sounded around them, and she slid her fangs from his skin. "It's a good thing your mother finally accepted her mate and moved in with him when he came a couple of days ago to visit with Parker."

Trigger let her nipple go with a pop, giving her a devilish grin. "True. She might frown on what we just did in the kitchen."

Alanna slowly shook her head, her eyes beginning to cloud over with an emotion he thought might be sorrow. She slid her arms around his neck, holding him to her as she whispered, "Distract me, Trigger. Please, I need you to distract me."

He knew what she meant. He could feel the dark emotions that were starting to swamp her through their bond. Jinx's emotions. Neither of them had any regrets about the decision they'd made to help the wolf, but Trigger knew it would be hard on his mate for a few days.

He lowered his lips to hers, giving her a soft, gentle kiss. "I've got you mate. I've always got you."

18

Alanna stood by the fireplace in the living room of their small cottage, her hand resting on the mantel as she stared into the flames, a soft smile on her lips. It was chilly, a bite of cold in the air that she wasn't used to this time of year. Trigger had started the fire for her even though he said he wouldn't normally do it for at least a couple more weeks. He didn't like the thought of her being cold and had already gone out and chopped extra firewood for her to use so she wouldn't run out if he was sent away on a mission.

The doorbell rang and she swung around in excitement. Trigger strode into the room, grinning over at her. "You ready for this?"

Was she ready? She'd been ready for weeks! "Open the door, Trigger!"

He laughed, shaking his head as he walked over to their front door. Grasping the doorknob, he swung it open, stepping back to let their visitors in.

Alanna's hand trembled as she raised it to cover her

mouth. Her eyes misted over with tears, and she couldn't stop the small sob that slipped out.

She was here. Sweet baby Nevaeh was in their home, alive and well according to her father. This would be the first time Alanna had seen her and Serenity since that night. The one that almost took the little one from all of them.

"Alanna? Are you okay?" Trigger quickly crossed the room to her and drew her into his arms. He ran his hand up and down her back, rubbing his cheek against hers, trying to sooth her.

She nodded, but the tears slipped free, flowing down her cheeks. She didn't even try to stop them.

"I've got you, mate." She knew he did. He always did.

Trigger held her close to him while Phoenix and Serenity unbundled the little girl. It was just shy of two months since the child was born. Just seven and a half short weeks. And while she was happy and healthy, she was still so small.

"Would you like to hold her?" Serenity asked softly, her own eyes wet with tears.

"Yes please." There was no other way to answer. The baby had a tight grip on her heart, and after what they'd gone through together Alanna knew she always would.

Trigger guided her over to the couch and lowered her down on it, sitting next to her. His arm stayed around her waist, supporting her, and she was grateful to him for it. She didn't know why she was so emotional, all she knew was that she felt as if her heart were about to pound right out of her chest.

Serenity lowered her daughter into Alanna's waiting arms, and Alanna was trembling so hard she prayed she didn't drop the child. Trigger slid an arm under the baby, helping Alanna brace her up. She smiled, realizing she should have known her mate would be there for her, the way he always was.

She looked down at the beautiful baby with all of her dark black hair. Her features were tiny and delicate, like a little babydoll. She was breathtaking. As she watched, the baby's lashes fluttered, her eyes opening, and Alanna gasped when she found herself staring into the most unique silver eyes she'd ever seen.

"Hello, little Vaeh. It's so wonderful to finally meet you."

The little girl stared at her for a moment, and then she smiled. A big, bright smile that lit up her face and caused those breathtaking eyes to glow.

"She knows you," Serenity whispered in shock. "She's never done that before. Smiled like that."

"We have a bond," Alanna admitted softly as she ran a finger lightly over the soft skin of the baby's cheek. "It was forged that night when I fought for her life. One that will never be broken. If she needs me, I will be there. Always. No questions asked. No matter what."

Phoenix knelt on the floor in front of them, and his mate dropped to her knees beside him. They both looked at her, their emotions so strong, Alanna immediately connected with them. They were grateful, happy, joyful. There was undying love for their child and a determination to keep her safe. But there was also a deep resolve to watch over Alanna and protect her from anyone or anything that threatened her in the future.

"You called her Vaeh?"

Alanna smiled at the little girl, leaning down to place a

kiss on her forehead. "Yes, she is Nevaeh, but one day she will be a warrior. So brave and powerful. Someone to look up to. Someone who will protect the innocent at all cost." Alanna raised her head to look at Phoenix and Serenity. "She will be a leader and will go by Vaeh."

"A leader?" Serenity whispered. "Like an alpha?"

Alanna dropped her gaze to the baby again and whispered, "No. Like a queen."

Make sure and visit my website for information on all of my books, and to sign up for my Newsletter where you will receive all of the latest information on new releases, sales, and more!

Website: **http://www.dawnsullivanauthor.com/**

I would love to have you join my reader's group, Author Dawn Sullivan's RARE Rebels, so that we can hang out and chat, and where you will also get sneak peeks of cover reveals, read excerpts before anyone else, and more!

https://www.facebook.com/groups/
AuthorDawnSullivansRebelReaders/

Dawn Sullivan

ABOUT THE AUTHOR

Dawn Sullivan has a wonderful, supportive husband, and three beautiful children. She enjoys spending time with them, which normally involves some baseball, shooting hoops, taking walks, watching movies, and reading.

Her passion for reading began at a very young age and only grew over time. Whether she was bringing home a book from the library, or sneaking one of her mother's romance novels to read by the light in the hallway when she was supposed to be sleeping, Dawn always had a book. She reads several different genres and subgenres, but Paranormal Romance and Romantic Suspense are her favorites.

Dawn has always made up stories of her own, and finally decided to start sharing them with others. She hopes everyone enjoys reading them as much as she enjoys writing them.

OTHER BOOKS BY DAWN SULLIVAN

RARE Series

Book 1 Nico's Heart

Book 2 Phoenix's Fate

Book 3 Trace's Temptation

Book 4 Saving Storm

Book 5 Angel's Destiny

Book 6 Jaxson's Justice

Book 7 Rikki's Awakening

White River Wolves Series

Book 1 Josie's Miracle

Book 2 Slade's Desire

Book 3 Janie's Salvation

Book 4 Sable's Fire

Serenity Springs Series

Book 1 Tempting His Heart

Book 2 Healing Her Spirit

Book 3 Saving His Soul

Book 4 A Caldwell Wedding

Book 5 Keeping Her Trust

Alluring Assassins

Book 1 Cassia

Sass and Growl

Book 1 His Bunny Kicks Sass

Book 2 Protecting His Fox's Sass

Book 3 Accepting His Witch's Sass

Book 4 Chasing His Lynx's Sass

Chosen By Destiny

Book 1 Blayke

Book 2 Bellame

Magical Mojo

Book 1 Witch Way To Love

Book 2 Witch Way To Jingle

Book 3 Witch Way To Cupid

Rogue Enforcers

Book 1 Karma

Book 2 Alayla

Book 3 Evalena

Book 4 Camryn

Book 5 Amira

Book 6 Edge

Dark Leopards East Texas Chapter

Book 1 Shadow's Revenge

Book 7 Demon's Hellfire

Book 10 Taz's Valor

Standalones

Wedding Bell Rock

Maid For Me

The De La Vega Familia Trilogy (Social Rejects Syndicate)

Book 1 Tomas

Book 2 Mateo

Book 3 Javier

Made in the USA
Coppell, TX
19 August 2024